A MESSY MURDER

A MESSY MURDER

Simon Brett

**SEVERN
HOUSE**

First world edition published in Great Britain and the USA in 2024
by Severn House, an imprint of Canongate Books Ltd,
14 High Street, Edinburgh EH1 1TE.

severnhouse.com

British Library Cataloguing-in-Publication Data
A CIP catalogue record for this title is available from the British Library.

ISBN-13: 978-1-4483-1103-3 (cased)
ISBN-13: 978-1-4483-1104-0 (e-book)

All Severn House titles are printed on acid-free paper.

MIX
Paper from
responsible sources
FSC   FSC® C013056
www.fsc.org

Typeset by Palimpsest Book Production Ltd.,
Falkirk, Stirlingshire, Scotland.
Printed and bound in Great Britain by TJ Books,
Padstow, Cornwall.

Praise for the Decluttering mysteries

About the author

Simon Brett worked as a producer in radio and television before taking up writing full-time. He is the author of more than 100 books, including the much-loved Fethering mysteries, the Mrs Pargeter novels and the Charles Paris detective series, as well as the Decluttering mysteries. In 2014, he was awarded the Crime Writers' Association's prestigious Diamond Dagger for sustained excellence and contribution to crime writing, and in the 2016 New Year's Honours he was awarded an OBE 'for services to literature'.

Married with three grown-up children, six grandchildren and a ginger cat called Douglas, he lives in an Agatha Christie-style village on the South Downs.

www.simonbrett.com

To
Marijke

ONE

I t wasn't the first dead body I had come across in the course of my work.

Nor, I am sad to say, was it the first time I'd discovered someone whose showed all the signs of being a suicide.

I'm Ellen Curtis, well into my fifties. I want to say post-menopausal, but my body can still surprise me with the occasional hot flush. Back when I had an operative womb, I gave birth to two children, Juliet (who calls herself Jools) and Ben. They're both in their twenties now.

The relevant body that I came across in the course of my work belonged to a man called Humphrey Carter. Oh, I haven't mentioned what my work is. I'm a professional declutterer. I run a company, rather winsomely called SpaceWoman. For most of the time I've been doing it, I've been a one-woman band. That has changed recently, though I'm not sure how long the change will continue.

Anyway, Humphrey Carter . . . If you were of a certain age, you'd have heard of him. Usually just called 'Humph'. Background as a journalist, presented a few programmes on television, then became a chat show host . . . though apparently he didn't like that description. He saw himself as a probing reporter, conducting one-to-one interviews with a single guest, rather than mixing up a bunch of showbiz types who'd just got a new film or song out.

He was frequently quoted in the press insisting that he was staying true to his journalistic roots. He would rather have *Humphrey Carter Interviews* . . . compared with John Freeman's *Face to Face* than Michael Parkinson's interview shows. He was constantly sniping at Parky, probably just jealous of the professional Yorkshireman's greater success. (Sorry, again, you may well not have heard of John Freeman. He developed a new intensive style of television interviewing in the 1950s. I never saw any of the shows but my mother Fleur Bonnier, an actress, kept complaining that she'd never been the subject of a 'Face to Face' interview with John Freeman. Which is typical of my mother's vanity. But don't worry, you'll hear more about her later.)

Humphrey Carter's heyday, I suppose, was the 1990s. Famed for his abrasive manner, a professional curmudgeon if you like, he started by interviewing politicians, before moving more into the world of showbusiness. At its peak, *Humphrey Carter Interviews . . .* attracted any guest who aspired to that uneasy title of 'celebrity'. Though the host still maintained his approach was that of 'a serious journalist'.

It came to a natural end with the development of other rival chat shows with younger hosts. Television is quite fickle about how long it allows presenters to stay in its spotlight. But, though no longer a regular fixture on the box, Humphrey Carter's career was by no means over. With his television-enhanced fame, he continued to guest on other programmes and his journalistic career revived. If a newspaper editor wanted a trenchant – not to say 'caustic' – commentary on some current issue, Humph was the go-to man for the job.

He also, like a lot of yesterday's television faces, continued to make a very good living from hosting corporate gigs, introducing in-house awards ceremonies, moderating panel discussions, after-dinner speaking . . . he was up for any of them and guaranteed to bring his own brand of grumpy efficiency to the proceedings. That side of his life was handled by one of the country's top television agents, who also dealt with celebrity speakers' bookings.

And, of course, Humph did charity work. He always claimed most of this was done anonymously but, remarkably, thanks to ambiguous references on social media to fundraising events he'd attended, everyone seemed to know about it.

Humph certainly regretted the end of his regular appearances on the box. He could become quite splenetic on the subject. I spent a little time on my own with him and had to listen to tirades about the short-sightedness of television executives and the incompetence of the hosts who had usurped his rightful place in the schedules. He was angry about the situation. And disappointed, yes.

But I wouldn't have said his disappointment about the decline in his career was a sufficient motive for him to take his own life.

But then, what did I know?

The approach which had led to my involvement with the Carter family had come through Humph's wife, Theresa. She'd just looked up online for declutterers round Chichester (known to the locals as 'Chi'), where I'm based, and randomly chosen SpaceWoman.

During the years of maximum television earning, the Carters had bought a house near Amberley, a village at the foot of the South Downs in West Sussex. Though not quite qualifying as a 'stately home', it was a substantial eight-bedroomed Victorian pile. And it was there that Humph and Theresa . . . well, I suspected, Theresa mostly . . . had brought up their daughters, Chloe and Kirsty.

The two girls having been off their hands for some years, the Carters decided they needed to downsize. And they'd accumulated so much stuff during their residence in Staddles – that was the house's name – that they needed some decluttering done before they put the house on the market.

I checked with Theresa that it was definitely decluttering she required. A lot of potential clients get in touch with SpaceWoman when all they want is basic house clearance. I tell them patiently that there are plenty of firms that do that, but I'm not one of them. My business is helping people to find space in their homes by deciding what they want to keep and what they want to dispose of.

Providing that service for people about to move, downsizing like the Carters, is not unusual.

Actually, when I say the Carters wanted to downsize, I don't think that's quite accurate. Theresa Carter wanted to downsize. Humph was, I'm sure, less keen on the idea. Again, that was not unusual in my profession. Almost by definition, every job I do involves me infiltrating a house where there is some level of dissension, if not actual conflict.

I gathered fairly quickly on my first encounter with both Carters that Theresa was the practical one. Whether that was in her nature,

I'm not sure, but I think living with Humph had forced her to take on the role. He was the famous one, he was the busier one, and life at Staddles revolved around him.

I was told quite soon that, when they met, she had been acting successfully on television and in the West End under the name of Theresa Burrows, but she'd put her career on hold to bring up the kids. That period of their lives had coincided with the sudden explosion of Humph's television success, and Theresa's career had never quite been taken off hold. She hadn't gone back to acting. It was Humph's assumption that she would take charge of everything domestic while he enjoyed his fame.

When I first saw Staddles, I realized what a burden being in charge of a place that size would be. Cleaners and gardeners could obviously help, but somebody had to make God knows how many daily decisions just to keep the whole show on the road.

It must also have been extremely expensive to run. Theresa had been honest with me from the start. Though nowhere near the breadline, their income had declined considerably from the glory days. When she told me this, she insisted that I shouldn't mention the financial imperative to Humph. He would 'take it badly'. So, for a good few reasons, it was no surprise that Theresa wanted to downsize.

In conversation, Humph supported that desire. Yes, he was as keen to downsize as his wife was. And yet his tone of voice and body language told the opposite story. Humphrey Carter, I soon recognized, was one of those men who used the demands of his work as a cover for innate laziness (and who could say what else?). He could see the arguments for downsizing, but he didn't actually want to take any action that would disturb the very pleasant pattern of his daily life. He liked having a big house in the country and a compact flat in Covent Garden.

He reckoned that, by giving vocal support to his wife's wishes and doing nothing, he could ensure that the proposed change didn't happen.

As I say, I'd worked out my analysis of Humphrey Carter's character pretty soon after meeting him. But I didn't know him well enough to recognize him as a suicide risk.

*   *   *

Maybe I should explain what I meant about no longer being a one-woman band. I'm a bit wary of the subject because I'm not sure how long it's going to last.

I mentioned my daughter Jools. Well, this bit is about her. Basically, for some years she worked in London in the fashion industry. Quite what she did there was never fully clear to me, but I think it was a kind of journalism. Not print, all online. And I think she became – or wanted to become – an 'influencer'.

My vagueness on the subject suggests that we weren't very close at the time, and I'm afraid that's true. Jools reacted to her father's death by clamming up. She didn't want to talk about him – or anything else that involved emotions.

So, I reconciled myself to a level of estrangement. I was sad, but I've never believed that shared DNA means that family members are automatically bonded. Jools seemed to be more in touch with her grandmother than she was with me. (My actress mother, Fleur, will undoubtedly crop up later on in this narrative. She doesn't like narratives in which she doesn't crop up.)

Anyway, I kind of went along with the way Jools wanted to play things. She seemed to have her life organized. I helped her with the deposit on a flat in Herne Hill and she repaid the money on the schedule we agreed. I also had no reason to believe that she wasn't up to date on her mortgage payments.

All fine and dandy . . . until she had some kind of breakdown. I won't go into the details now. Suffice to say that Jools ended up back at my house in Chichester and, at least for the time being, she's on the staff at SpaceWoman. Currently, a two-woman band.

Which is working out better than I would ever have thought possible.

I should also give you an update on my son, Ben. He's currently in the States, pursuing his career as an animator. Very successfully, I believe. I say that because I don't hear much from him. That could be good news or it could be bad news. It could mean he's having such a wild time that he hasn't got time to contact his old Ma. Or it could be because he's feeling so low that he doesn't want to contact anyone.

Ben inherited his father Oliver's depressive streak. Which means I'm never going to not worry about him.

*   *   *

But back to Humphrey Carter's suicide . . .

I'd been doing the Staddles job on my own. Jools was working on a students' house in Worthing. The parents of the four residents had been so appalled that they had clubbed together to pay SpaceWoman to alleviate the squalor in which their offspring were living. An unusual commission but, in my experience, not unprecedented.

The fact that I trusted Jools to work independently was a measure of my growing confidence in her abilities. She had resources of empathy and patience, particularly with younger clients, which I would never have imagined from her. And which were certainly better than mine. Though I dared not make predictions, it boded well for our future collaboration.

I'd started working at Staddles the previous Monday. I had other jobs on, but it was agreed I'd go back there on the Friday. When I'd first arrived, only Theresa had been there. Humph was up in London, having what he called 'meetings', but his wife described as 'boozy lunches with old cronies, more likely'. And, with just the two of us, we did make quite a lot of progress.

Without knowing exactly what property the Carters were going to downsize into, there was guesswork involved but it was hard to underestimate the scale of decluttering required. Any house in which a family has lived for over thirty years is going to accumulate a lot of stuff. And if it's an eight-bedroomed Victorian number, the stuff expands accordingly.

(Incidentally, I always use the word 'stuff' for what people accumulate in their homes. It's somehow less judgemental than 'rubbish' or even 'clutter'. After all, everyone has stuff in their life. And most of us have some stuff we don't want other people to know about. Maybe that's the reason I continue to make a living.)

In the course of my work for SpaceWoman, I have encountered a wide variety of difficult clients, but I'm glad to say Theresa Carter did not fit into that category. Still retaining the slender frame, fine bone structure and blonde hair (surely no longer unaided) which had wowed the West End in her twenties, she was a refreshingly practical woman. I nearly used the word 'sensible' there, but for me that always sounds slightly derogatory, conjuring up images of 'sensible shoes' and sickeningly reasonable right-wing newspaper columnists.

Theresa was also easy to get along with. I'd warmed to her voice when we talked on the phone and meeting her in the flesh did nothing to change that first impression.

On the Monday, over good coffee in a huge, high-ceilinged kitchen whose Aga defied the February cold, we worked out our plan of attack. It was a situation I had been in many times before, but Theresa very quickly caught on to the basic principles of decluttering.

I always tend to start with the obvious. Every house, except for one that is welcoming its first owners, is full of stuff that needs getting rid of. It's just that no one has summoned up the energy to load a car and take it down to the dump. And after a time, you stop noticing stuff that is in obvious need of removal.

I refer to chairs that never got mended, baby baths and infant cots that were outgrown, leaking wellies, outdated electronic equipment that got consigned to the back of cupboards, never-to-be-worn-again clothes stuffed into drawers . . . the list goes on.

Theresa and I agreed that we'd do a cull of that lot right through Staddles and pile it up in one of the old stables until there was enough for a truckload to be taken to the recycling centre. The transportation side of the job I would hand over to my friend Dodge, who drove a punctiliously maintained 1951 Morris Commer CV9/40 Tipper van and whose services I had used on many previous occasions.

The next stage of our decluttering, I suggested to Theresa, would move on to the stuff that was still viable and might be of use to someone other than the Carter family. This could be sold, given to friends or donated to charity.

For this category, we didn't move anything at that point, just assessed it. Some candidates for disposal were uncontentious. Beds in particular. If the downsizing turned out to be from eight bedrooms to four, say, there were some that wouldn't be needed but could have a useful life somewhere else.

What was contentious was the personal stuff. Theresa said some of that might need delicate negotiation. Contents of the two girls' bedrooms, for example. She wasn't the first mother who'd found that, though her offspring lived lives of fashionable minimalism elsewhere, they were very resistant to the idea of their stuff being removed from the family home. Though I was prepared to back her up with logistical arguments, she would have to take the lead in dealing with her daughters.

The same went for any negotiation with Humph. His work area was on the second floor at the front of the house, commanding lavish views over the South Downs. It looked like a stage set from a time when West End plays about writers – like *Sleuth* – always gave them impossibly glamorous studies to work in.

I met him on the Friday. In his study, which was clearly his domain, even part of his personality. And it was amazingly full of stuff. But I didn't see the untidiness of someone disorganized or losing control. Messy but artfully messy. This, it seemed to say, is the space of someone bursting with energy and ideas. These books and documents and scraps of paper are not scattered randomly. They are spread about for the convenience of me, Humphrey Carter, so that I instantly access my research materials for the next project. This is the study of a very busy and successful man.

Theresa introduced us. Though he had put on a lot of weight, I recognized the Humphrey Carter of his television heyday. The hair was no longer black and short, He had grown it and added a messianic beard, both steel grey. He greeted me with the finesse of a professional charmer. I recognized the artifice but couldn't stop myself from thinking that he did do charm rather well. He had perfected that trick of locking eyes and making you feel he was concentrating all his attention on you.

I was trying to work out his age from what I knew of his career history when Theresa supplied the answer for me.

'Sorry, I must get back to the kitchen,' she said. 'Lot of cooking to do. We have a big weekend coming up, Ellen.'

'Oh?'

'Humph will be eighty on Sunday.'

He preened himself, stroking his hair and beard. 'You'd never think it, would you?'

'No' seemed to be the only thing to say.

'Of course, these days they say that eighty is the new forty.'

He chuckled fruitily. 'Load of cobblers, but certain old dogs may still have life in them.'

This again was delivered to me in the full beam of his concentration. Which vanished quickly as he turned to Theresa and almost snapped, 'When are the girls coming?'

'This evening. Eight at the earliest. Chloe's filming all day, then Kirsty and Garth are going to give the kids supper and put them in their night things, so that they can be shovelled straight into bed when they get here.'

'Are you having a big party?' I asked.

'Major lunch on Sunday.' Theresa didn't sound as if it was an entirely welcome thought. 'Family, friends . . .'

'And copious amounts of very good Bordeaux,' said Humph with a Rabelaisian laugh.

Nothing was said during that meeting about the decluttering of the study. Now I'd met its occupant, I was ever more aware of the delicacy with which that part of the project would have to be approached. I must move cautiously, in close consultation with Theresa.

And put the study low down the list. It wasn't as if I hadn't got lots of other things to do at Staddles. So, I spent that Friday going through the house and making lists on my iPad of stuff that could have a future life elsewhere once the downsizing actually happened. I kept having to go into the kitchen, where Theresa was engaged in lavish and elaborate cooking, to consult her about the fate of various items.

By the end of the day, I had a working strategy of how the contents of Staddles could be humanely culled.

When I left, Humph insisted on coming downstairs to say goodbye. A slathering of politesse, as ever. I think he wanted to ensure that I left the premises thinking about him. He was ridiculously vain, but I still couldn't help acknowledging that he did have a lot of charm.

The agreement with Theresa was that I should next come on the Monday. She felt sure that, after the excesses of his birthday lunch, which would continue all day on the Sunday, Humph wouldn't be getting up very early the next day. Theresa reckoned, if I arrived about eight, I could get in at least an hour of planning how to declutter the study before he went in there.

She gave me a front door key, so that I didn't need to disturb anyone when I arrived.

On the Sunday, I had lunch with my mother Fleur (a gruelling assignment whose details I won't go into right now) and the next morning relished the start of a new week.

I left home in good time to arrive at Staddles by eight o'clock. I drive a blue Yeti, a Skoda which pretends to be an SUV but doesn't have the horsepower to justify the claim. The SpaceWoman logo is printed across the back door. I was, as ever, wearing my work kit, dark leggings, stout trainers and a blue polo shirt, also with the logo woven into it.

When I drove into the broad gravel drive, there were a couple of cars there that I didn't recognize. Probably guests who'd stayed over from the birthday lunch, family maybe. But there didn't seem to be much sign of life from inside the house.

I let myself in and went straight up to the study to devise a plan of campaign for its decluttering. I had expected, from what Theresa had said, that the place would be empty.

It wasn't. Humphrey Carter lay slumped forward over his desk. Dead. With an empty bottle of Famous Grouse lying sideways close by.

Also, on the desk, with a damp yellow whisky stain on it, was a page from an old magazine. A ragged edge down the right-hand side showed where it had been torn out. It was a full-page article entitled 'COME IN, NUMBER EIGHTY – YOUR TIME IS UP! by Humphrey Carter'.

This is what I read:

> Do you remember when everyone used to maunder on about 'built-in obsolescence'? Basically, it was the principle by which products were manufactured with basic design weaknesses which meant they'd soon break down and need replacement. It was the dynamo behind the growth of many multinational corporations and is very much still with us. Does everyone actually need to own the latest model computer? They wouldn't if the devices

weren't updated with minimal changes on an annual basis.

But what the right-on people who moaned worthily about being taken for a ride by Big Tech didn't seem to realize was that they were living inside the archetype of 'built-in obsolescence'. The human body.

Yup, we've all got one and nobody's got one that's immune from deterioration. Bits drop off. Not so much in the early years, but as time starts to accelerate, the drop-off rate accelerates with it. And while some bits, like hips and knees, you can get replaced, there are other bits which are, as yet, irreplaceable.

What's particularly galling is that the bits that drop off are always things associated with pleasure. The muscles that used to celebrate the pure joy of movement stiffen or go flabby. Appendixes start to grumble, bowels become irritable. It takes more drink to reach the happy stage of inebriation and frequently the happy stage is bypassed altogether on the road to a hangover. The magic wands of sexual fulfilment grow slack and flaccid. Aneurisms swell and cancers spread.

It's a one-way street, getting old, and the destination is somewhere no one wants to go to. Different vehicles may travel faster or slower but, ultimately, we're all on the same bus route.

Which is very wasteful, apart from anything else. I'm not entirely committed to those people who pontificate right-eously about saving the planet, but I can see the logic of some redistribution of assets. How much of the medical budget, certainly in developed countries, is spent on mini-mally extending the lives of the wealthy elderly? What volume of human resources is dedicated to nursing and caring for them? What investment in laundry services is put into cleaning and recleaning their soiled sheets?

The introduction of a legal lifespan limit for the elderly would solve all of these problems at a stroke (unless, of course, a stroke gets them before they reach the limit). And the money saved could be used to delay the man-made destruction of our planet. There's a logic to satisfy the most rabid of eco-warriors.

The question is, of course, at what point should this merciful final step be taken. Many people argue that we have much to learn from the old, but that's really crap. Nobody over eighty has ever done anything very useful for the world. The aged have lingered on, irritating and bankrupting their descendants who, whatever sentiments they piously intone, would feel nothing about the ancient relative's demise except relief.

'Three score and ten' is the biblical recommendation. Well, let's be generous, given advances in medical science, and boost that up to 'three score and twenty' . . . or 'four score', if you prefer. Other lifespans have been arbitrarily imposed in dystopian science fiction, but I still think the right cut-off point is eighty.

Eighty years old. Quite long enough for anyone to live. In the cause of humankind, at the age of eighty everyone should opt for voluntary euthanasia.

When you make the public-spirited decision to do it, avoid complications and pain. Cosset yourself. Don't mess with car crashes, ropes or stones in your pockets at the seaside. Use poison. Not one of those stomach-griping poisons like arsenic, cyanide or strychnine. No, no, use sleeping pills. Just take too many of them . . . and slip away.

Have a drink to help the medicine go down. A drink you like. A drink you like very much. Make your last recollections ones of enjoyment. Maybe that really nice Châteauneuf-du-Pape you've been saving for a 'special occasion'. What occasion could me more special than your departure from this life?

I must confess my sleeping-pill-accompanying drink of choice would not be a wine. I like wine but I've always found that, for getting pissed, spirits are more effective. So, it'd be whisky for me. And not some posh, esoteric single malt. No, I'm not up myself. A common or garden blended whisky would do the job. Famous Grouse is the one I favour. I have very frequently fallen asleep following excesses of that. What more suitable tipple could there be to escort me into that magical sleep from which I do not wake?

Come on, everyone, don't be greedy. Give a thought to the younger generation. Support voluntary euthanasia at eighty. You know it makes sense.

TWO

'Ah. I'm sorry.'

Theresa Carter stood in the doorway, a dark blue dressing gown over her nightwear.

'He does this rather often,' she went on. 'Last thing at night he says there's something he needs to check in here . . . by which I know he means the Famous Grouse . . . and I find him like this in the morning. I'll wake him up.'

'I'm afraid you won't,' I said.

Theresa was clearly shocked at her husband's death but something, possibly her training as an actor or just innate self-discipline, did not allow her to show too much overt emotion. Or maybe it was my presence, someone she didn't know very well, that made her control her grief.

After she had confirmed that Humph was dead and glanced at the magazine article, she said, 'I must tell Chloe. Coffee in the kitchen in a quarter of an hour.'

I suggested, 'Maybe I should just go . . .'

'If you don't mind, I'd rather you stayed, Ellen. I don't want to be on my own at the moment.'

What that said about her relationship with her daughter I didn't like to question.

'Besides, I'm afraid the police are going to have to be called and, you, as the person who found his body . . .'

'Yes, of course I'll stay,' I said.

'I'm sorry you've had to get involved in this,' she said. 'It must be a terrible shock for you.'

My thought was that it must have been an even bigger shock for her. But that wasn't what I said. 'It's all right, Theresa. I've seen dead bodies before.'

'Yes.' My words had prompted some memory in her. 'Oh, were you the declutterer . . .? There was a case I read about in the papers . . . in Chichester . . . some old recluse who'd been poisoned . . . and it was the declutterer who proved it was murder . . . Was that you?'

Since she seemed to know all the facts about the killing of Cedric Waites, I couldn't deny my involvement.

'So, are you a kind of private investigator, Ellen?'

'Hardly,' I said. But the question made me wonder. I did seem to be increasingly caught up in cases of suspicious behaviour. 'No, no, of course I'm not,' I added firmly.

'Coffee.'

With that single word, Theresa left the study, straight-backed, still in control. I wondered if she'd manage to fit a few surreptitious tears into the quarter of an hour break she had decreed.

I used the time for further inspection of the scene of death. I also got out the mobile phone to take some photographs.

Including one of the magazine article.

'Typical of bloody Daddy,' said Chloe. 'Turning his own death into a media circus.'

'It isn't a media circus,' said her mother quietly.

'It will be. He will have ensured that it is. Probably posted the details on social media.'

'He wouldn't have done that,' said Theresa.

'How do you know?'

'Because Humph had recently cut himself off from all social media.'

'Why?'

'Too much criticism. He'd post his opinions, loudly and brashly, as ever. But he didn't like it when anonymous people hit back at him, calling him a has-been. So, ever the one to avoid criticism when he could, Humph backed off, said he was bored with social media, and stopped using it,' Theresa concluded.

'Really?' said her daughter, to whom, like anyone of her generation, the idea of conducting a life without social media was bizarre and incongruous.

Chloe Carter looked vaguely familiar. Theresa had mentioned something about her following her father's career path, so perhaps I'd seen her on some television programme. Not prime time, though. And, because of SpaceWoman commitments, I hardly ever watch daytime television. (I don't think I would if I wasn't working, actually. What I've seen of it hasn't impressed me.)

The girl, probably in her late thirties, had inherited her mother's slenderness and fine bones but her dark colouring was all Humph. She contrived to be, at the same time, stunning and combative. Not a woman to cross.

'Do you want to go up and see him?' asked Theresa gently.

'No, I bloody don't! He spent his entire life upstaging me. I'm not interested in how he's tried to upstage me in death.'

'Don't overdramatize, Chloe.'

'I am not overdramatizing anything. You know how Daddy always diminished my achievements. The same way he did with yours. Any professional success I had was always played down. He never encouraged me. He didn't like anything that threatened to shift the spotlight away from him. I'm glad he's dead.'

It was a strange conversation for me to be witnessing. I felt sure Chloe's vehemence was a cover for more complex reactions to her father's death. And what was going on behind Theresa's genteel façade remained difficult to fathom.

The police had been called. On the phone, they had said nothing should be touched in the study until they had inspected the scene. The tableau in the kitchen, while we awaited their arrival, was slightly incongruous, the three of us sitting round the table drinking coffee. I felt like an interloper in the family tragedy but was also aware how much Theresa needed me to be there.

Chloe Carter looked challengingly at her mother. 'Go on. You've got to do it.'

'I know I have. I just don't feel I can at the moment.'

Chloe shrugged. 'Well . . .' Then she said, sharply. 'Do you want me to do it?'

'No, no! I hate to think what you'd say, but I know it wouldn't be the right approach.'

Another shrug. 'You can't keep on cossetting her. She has to come to terms with the real world. I know she claims to be happy in her little married cocoon with the two beautiful children and that waste-of-a-space of a husband, but she can't be protected from unpleasant events all her bloody life.'

I had by now worked out that Chloe was talking about her sister.

'Yes, I know.' Theresa looked very stressed now. 'But it's just
. . . Kirsty was always so close to Humph.'

'Yes, Daddy's little girl. She played up to him like a little tart
from the moment she was born. Never disagreed with him, thought
he could do no wrong, thought his farts smelled of roses.'

'I'm not denying any of that, Chloe. But the fact remains that
hearing he's dead is going to upset Kirsty very much.'

'OK, what if it does? Would you rather she heard it on the
lunchtime news?'

'But, surely, nobody knows yet?'

'Don't you believe it. Daddy didn't have the kind of profile
he had in his prime, but he was still a minor celebrity. If he
didn't do it on social media, he probably flagged up his forth-
coming suicide to some of his old Fleet Street cronies. His final
coup de théâtre?'

Theresa didn't look as if she wanted to consider this possibility.
'I'll phone Kirsty after the police have arrived,' she said firmly.

That prompted another shrug from her daughter. An outsider
might have been surprised that the two of them were having such
a personal conversation with another person present, but I wasn't.
It's happened before. Quite often. I've heard clients reveal
amazing secrets. It's as if they forget I'm there. I don't think this
invisibility is an aspect of my character. The nature of my work
often puts me together with people at moments of extreme stress
when they lose their usual caution.

I broke the silence. 'I hope you don't mind my asking, Theresa,
but did you recognize the article on your husband's desk?'

The new widow nodded. 'Yes. I'd completely forgotten about
it, though. Written a long time ago.'

'I couldn't see the name of the magazine it was published in.'

'*Rant.*' She smiled wryly. 'Which was a very good description
of its contents. Needless to say, a natural home for the opinions
of someone like Humph.'

'Ah.'

'He used to write for *Punch* sometimes, though he thought its
editorial policy was a bit pussyfooted. When *Punch* finally folded,
Humph and a few like-minded provocateurs set up *Rant*. Only
lasted a few months. They hadn't got the financial support they
needed and also wildly overestimated the number of people who

were going to buy the thing. Ranting didn't prove to be as popular as they had hoped.'

'But what he wrote in that article . . . about voluntary euthanasia . . . did you think it expressed his actual views?'

'No, I thought it was just another piece Humph wrote to amuse and infuriate his readers in equal measure, something of a speciality of his.' For the first time, Theresa Carter's carapace of calm was threatened. 'But now,' she said, 'what else is there to think?'

Shortly after that, Chloe went off to her room, saying she had 'work calls to make'. In our short acquaintance, I had got the impression she would fall back on that imperative a lot. Her work was far more important than mere domestic issues, like a suicide in the family. A sense of priorities she shared with her late father. And the fact that he regarded his work as so much more important than hers was one of the roots of their antagonism.

The police seemed to be taking a long time to arrive. Theresa's well-bred presentation of herself was beginning to feel the strain. She couldn't stay seated for long, kept getting up and walking twitchily around the kitchen. I thought she'd probably feel better if she gave in to some of the emotions that must have been crowding in on her. But it wasn't my place to say that.

What I did say was, 'Look, if you want to call Kirsty, I'll happily go into another room while you do it.'

'No, no, it's fine. I'll wait till after the police have been. I'll probably have more to tell her then.'

A silence. Then, from me, tentatively, 'Theresa, do you mind my asking how Humph seemed yesterday? I mean, for the birthday lunch. Did he give any indication of what he might be planning?'

That prompted a short, hard laugh. 'God, no. He was his typical loud-mouthed self, glorying – as ever – in being the centre of attention. Drinking hugely, and that went on through the evening and into the night. After a skinful of the Bordeaux, he always found comfort in a bottle of Famous Grouse.' She realized what she'd said and her poise was momentarily threatened. 'Or . . . he found something in a bottle of Famous Grouse.'

'You suggested earlier that it wasn't unusual for him to fall asleep in his study and still be there in the morning.'

'No, it wasn't. Mind you, he usually had to wake up to pee and he'd quite often come back to bed after that.'

Having explored the whole house on my decluttering mission, I knew that Theresa and Humph still shared a double bed. But it certainly wasn't my place – or indeed the right time – for me to enquire further about their married life.

Thinking of motives for suicide, I asked, 'Did Humph ever worry about drinking too much?'

'No, he gloried in it. He always had drunk too much. He was drinking too much when I first met him. Mind you, so was I back then. Early years of our married life, we hardly drew a sober breath. I cut back a bit when the girls came along, but not Humph. By no means. He'd grown up in a drinking culture. Journalism, television, theatre. Back then people weren't sipping their sedate Perriers. They were straight round the pub at opening time . . . back when pubs weren't open all day.

'Humph's of the generation that boast about their drinking. A dinosaur in so many ways. It was a badge of honour for him. Whenever anyone mentioned the government's "recommended guidelines", he'd go into a rant about the "nanny state". It was almost as if he was challenging medical opinion. Saying, "Look at me. I drink far more than I'm told I should and I'm absolutely fine."'

'And was he always absolutely fine?' I asked.

'How do you mean?'

'Did he have any long-term illnesses?'

'No. He's always been disgustingly healthy. Well, that is, until now . . .' Her equilibrium was once again under threat but she brushed the thought away. 'Oh, he had coughs and colds and, when he did, he had them in a totally masculine fashion.'

'Man flu?'

'Exactly. No, you'd have thought he'd got bubonic plague symptoms. Under piles of duvets, snuffling, moaning, chain-drinking whisky toddies. Making himself the centre of attention yet again,' she concluded ruefully.

'And had he seen a doctor recently?'

'Why do you ask?'

'Well, I was just thinking . . . if he'd been to the doctor . . .

and been given some bad news that he didn't want to tell you about . . .?'

'Ah. I'm with you. A motive for . . .' Theresa couldn't say the words '. . . for what happened.'

'Yes.'

'Humph hadn't been to the doctor's surgery in the past five years . . . probably longer . . . except to have his flu jabs.'

I couldn't help probing a bit further. 'So, it was just family, was it, at the birthday lunch yesterday?'

'Family, plus our friend Niall.'

'Oh?'

'Humph's known him forever. He was the executive producer on *Humphrey Carter Interviews* . . . And I've known him even longer than that.' She responded to my quizzical look. 'We were at RADA together. Along with Zena, who became Niall's wife. Then he moved away from acting into production. Zena and I continued in the theatre . . . well, I did till I had the kids.' There was no resentment as she said this, but a kind of ruefulness.

'You've probably heard of Zena, actually, Ellen,' she went on. 'Zena Fitzpatrick.'

'Oh yes. Seen her in lots of television stuff. But didn't I read somewhere that she . . .?'

'Yes, she died, nearly six months ago now. Lung cancer. Too many stage-fright-quenching cigarettes. We were all devastated because our girls virtually grew up with Niall and Zena's boys. Even Humph seemed mildly shaken.

'Anyway, so Niall was here. He's still totally lost without Zena. You never quite know what goes on inside another marriage. I thought there might be cracks but, seeing how devastated Niall is . . . Well, shows how much I know. So, he was here, trying, as ever, to keep pace with Humph's drinking. And, inevitably—'

The doorbell rang. It was the police, finally.

I did my civic duty and answered all the questions they put to me. I said I'd be happy to sign a statement. They took my contact details and told me I could leave.

I had the briefest of parting words with Theresa. She was still maintaining her remarkable outward serenity. Maybe she was deferring her emotional collapse until she had talked to her younger daughter.

She said she'd be in touch about the decluttering 'when things have settled down a bit'. But I wondered whether I would ever hear from her again. At some point she was going to feel the full impact of what had happened and then I might be all too potent a reminder of the tragedy.

I sat in the Yeti on the gravel in front of Staddles, working on my mobile, rearranging my schedule, now I had the unexpected bonus of a free half-day.

And I thought my dealings with the Carter family were at an end.

It wasn't the first time I'd been wrong about something like that.

THREE

'He's got to have tests,' announced my mother down the phone, in full drama queen mode.

'Are you talking about Kenneth?'

'Ellen, of course I'm talking about Kenneth.'

Fleur Bonnier is primarily an actress (though, when in conversation with younger members of her profession, she describes herself as an 'actor'). And when I say 'primarily', that's exactly what I mean. Being an actress is the dominant ingredient in her personality. Certainly, much more important to her than being a mother. Once her theatrical friends lost interest in the bravery and novelty (back then) of her bringing up a child on her own, Fleur lost interest in me. She never let me be unaware that my mere presence was an impediment to the full realization of her career potential.

'What's happened?' I asked.

'Kenneth had to have an MOT with the quack. You know, one of those regular check-ups when you reach a certain age.'

Her vagueness reminded me of a bind my mother had got herself into. When she first got together with Kenneth, she made much of the fact that he was younger than her, even – I still shrivel at the recollection – describing him as her 'toyboy'. But after a celebration at the golf club of his seventieth birthday, she changed tack. Drawing attention to the fact that she was older than someone whose age was so publicly known wasn't good for her self-image. All of a sudden, she became studiedly vague about the age difference between them.

'So,' I said, 'this was a seventy-year-old NHS check with the GP?'

'No, Ellen. Kenneth went private. As a successful solicitor, he's got very good health insurance.'

'I'm sure he has. Anyway, what was it that came up?'

'Blood pressure,' Fleur announced dramatically.

'Not unusual at his age. And there are lots of medications around for it.'

'Ah, but Kenneth is already on all the medications. Has been for years. Which is why they've referred him for tests.'

'Do you know what the tests are for?'

'Well, blood pressure, obviously.'

'Yes, but do you know any more detail?'

'No. Doctors never tell you anything.'

I was reminded that Fleur believes the whole medical profession is a conspiracy devoted to not taking her health issues seriously.

'When does Kenneth have the tests?'

'Tomorrow.'

'I'm sure he'll be fine.'

'Oh, it's easy for you to say that and leave me to take all the burden of worry on myself.'

Sometimes, it is just not worth responding to my mother's emotional blackmail. Quite often, actually.

'Anyway, Fleur, I must be getting on. It's a working day, you know.'

'Oh. Of course. So, how's the cleaning going?'

My mother cherishes an extensive list of subjects, which are regularly raised with the sole purpose of annoying me. An old favourite is her deliberate misunderstanding the nature of my work at SpaceWoman. There's no point in putting her right when she refers to it as 'cleaning'. The fact that I've reacted to the trigger word will only encourage her. What I find particularly annoying is that, however many times she says it, I still get annoyed.

'Fine, thank you,' I replied, without intonation.

'And is Jools still working for you?'

A curt 'Yes' from me.

'I do think it's such a pity that a girl with such potential should end up doing cleaning. Jools had a very promising career in the fashion world, you know.'

Another trigger point to which I am not going to react. 'Anyway, I must get on,' I said again.

'Oh yes. Of course, cleaning's much more important than providing moral support to your mother when she's worried about her husband.'

Again, just not worth going into battle on that one.

Fleur shifted her point of attack to another of her recurring irritants. 'Have you heard anything from Ben recently?'

'No. Which I'm sure means everything in the States is completely fine.' If only I could feel as sure of that as I sounded.

'Oh yes, I expect so,' said Fleur. 'And he certainly needed to spread his wings a bit, didn't he?'

I couldn't stop myself from asking, 'What do you mean by that?'

'Oh, just that he always was tied a bit too tightly to Mummy's apron strings, wasn't he?'

That one I was not going to rise to either. Yes, Ben probably had spent more time at home with me than most men in their early twenties do, but that was because of his fragile mental health. Mention that to Fleur, though, and it was only a matter of time before she would say that her generation had had too many 'real problems' to have time for being depressed. And that Ben should 'snap out of it'.

If she said that, I would not be responsible for what I might say back to her. I left it at, 'I'll be sure to tell you when I do hear from him. Now, I really must—'

'And what about Jools?' she wheedled. 'We used to be such chums and I hardly seem to hear from her now.'

'She's fine, as well,' I said tersely.

'Have you found out yet what happened while she was in London?'

'No, I haven't.'

'Well, have you asked her?'

'No. The right moment hasn't come up.'

'Huh. If I'd spent my life waiting for "the right moment" to come up, my career would never have got anywhere.' Fleur was full of annoying little nuggets of folk wisdom like that.

'Anyway, I'm sorry, I must go. I'll call you later in the week. And I'm sure Kenneth will be fine. Bye.'

I put the phone down.

As I hurried out to the Yeti, I felt troubled. After more than fifty years of being Fleur Bonnier's daughter, I really shouldn't still let her get to me. But she does. She knows my triggers too well.

She knows I'm worried about the deafening silence from Ben the other side of the Atlantic.

She knows I'm worried about Jools, too. My daughter had been through some kind of breakdown when I rescued her from her flat in Herne Hill and brought her back to Chichester. And it's true, since then I haven't found 'the right moment' to ask her about the background to that event. It's partly cowardice on my part. My daughter and I are getting on better now than we have done any time since Oliver's death. Working together for SpaceWoman is turning out better than I ever imagined it could. Jools is demonstrating great efficiency and unexpected levels of empathy with the clients. I don't want to threaten that fragile harmony.

The other disquieting content in Fleur's call was the news about Kenneth. Though I breezily assured her everything would be fine, it did make me think about what she'd be like without him on the scene.

Kenneth is a person I neither like nor dislike. He's a solicitor who keeps talking about cutting his workload down to three days a week, but never seems to do anything about it. So, most of the time, he's either in the office or, at weekends, playing golf. I wouldn't know whether it's true, but Fleur keeps implying, with excruciating coyness, that they still have an active sex life.

Though Kenneth's schedule means they don't see a lot of each other, Fleur does get quite a charge from being married. He's well-heeled too, and she enjoys the freedom of his credit cards. Also, after a fairly rackety and varied relationship history – including a brief dalliance with my actor father, who I only met once, in my teens – marriage to Kenneth has given her a level of respectability that she hasn't enjoyed before. And, though she'd denounce such a lifestyle to her theatre friends as 'hope-lessly bourgeois', she actually quite likes it.

All I can keep thinking, though, is that, should Kenneth shuffle off this mortal coil, his widow would become even more dependent on her daughter.

Which is not a prospect said daughter relishes.

I was surprised, in the week after it, how relatively little coverage there was of Humphrey Carter's death. Oh, it made the radio bulletins the day it was announced. A few broadcasters of the same vintage were wheeled out to recall encounters with the deceased which mostly involved alcohol and didn't improve with the telling.

The television news programmes made mention of his death but kept their tributes short. In a medium of such fickle memories, someone doesn't have to be off the screen for long to be totally forgotten. Humphrey Carter was very definitely 'yesterday's man'.

The newspaper obituaries were respectful but less than effusive. Which I found a little odd. Journalists usually make a disproportionate amount of fuss when one of their own dies. They think their profession is much more important than what anyone else does, and award column inches accordingly. But that didn't seem to have happened with Humph.

And then I realized why. He'd gone to telly. He hadn't stayed in the hothouse of print journalism. He'd taken the thirty pieces of silver on offer and gone away to make much more money than his journalistic contemporaries. It was jealousy that restrained the generosity of his obituaries.

I couldn't help thinking how disappointed Humphrey Carter would have been by the lukewarm reaction to his death. His ego would have demanded more, much more.

But also, he must have seen it coming. He must have experienced many minor humiliations in the professional arena, which signalled the diminishing interest the media had in him.

For a man who had thrived all his life on being the centre of attention, the cumulative effect of that process might have become a motive for suicide.

Interestingly, though, that last word was not mentioned in any of the coverage. Whoever was controllingly the flow of information to the media was doing a good job.

As you've probably gathered by now, being a declutterer involves handling a lot of stuff. And, by now, I know instinctively where most of that stuff should go. For the stuff that has no resale value, it's the recycling centre. For the stuff from which the owner wants to raise money, I have an automatic recall of all the South Coast's antique sellers and junk shops. (Of which there are many. Not for nothing is the area nicknamed the 'Costa Geriatrica'. There's a high death rate among the elderly, and most surviving family members' sole aim is to get rid of the deceased relative's belongings and get their house on the market as soon as possible.)

Books, incidentally, are a special case. It's dispiriting how often they're all chucked out without even being looked at. Most, of course, go to the house clearance people and I hate to think of what happens to them then. When I end up decluttering books, I do check them through and take the ones that aren't falling apart to Oxfam. Every now and then, I get a call back from them saying something I delivered turned out to be really valuable. That's a good feeling.

I have an automatic recall of all the other local charities. This is more interesting for me, and I often try to persuade my clients – assuming they're not actually destitute – to send their unwanted belongings somewhere where they can do a bit of good. There are some charities which are basically just second-hand furniture stores. Donated goods are sold to raise money for rough sleepers, recently released prisoners, women's refuges and causes like that.

There are others where the goods themselves are repurposed. Even on the supposedly prosperous South Coast of England there are families living without basic essentials like beds. I have seen many times the gratitude of people in such circumstances, for whom donated furniture can be literally life-changing.

There are also focused charities working with deprived children who are crying out for discarded sports equipment.

And then, for some very specific kinds of stuff, there's Dodge.

In all the time I've known Dodge, he's never once looked me in the eye, but I like to think he regards me as a friend. He has a complex history, of which I have only been able to piece together parts. Early career as a City whizz-kid making huge amounts of dosh. Then some kind of breakdown, from which he emerged profoundly anti-consumerism. I've a feeling drugs were involved in his crack-up and, although he keeps very quiet about it, I know that he volunteers as a counsellor at some rehabilitation centre for addicts in Portsmouth.

He always dresses in clothes so old and worn that it's difficult to know what colour they started out as. Since I've known him, he hasn't been in a relationship or expressed any interest in being in one. I've a feeling there may have been a woman – even a wife – involved before his breakdown, but that's only a conjecture on my part. He's never mentioned anything about it.

Dodge owns what used to be a farmhouse and some outbuildings near Walberton. I don't know if he bought the place with money salvaged from his City career or inherited it from his parents. There is so much I don't know about Dodge.

He doesn't live in the house. That's where he stores all the pallets and other stuff he accumulates for recycling. He actually sleeps and eats in one of the outbuildings which he has converted into a workshop. There he makes furniture out of materials he's salvaged from skips and fly-tipping sites and the seashore. Though he occasionally has to go the hardware store for nails and other ironmongery, I've never known him pay for any wood.

It was because of wood that I was at his place that Monday afternoon. Though the SpaceWoman blue Yeti is not a large car, it has a capacious space at the back. With the seats down, I can store a surprising amount. At the end of the previous week, I had done a job for a widow who wanted to reorganize the space in her bungalow, following her husband's death. As I spent more time with her it became clear that what she actually wanted to do was to obliterate every sign that the deceased had ever lived there.

Which meant getting rid of all his books. As a retired history teacher, he'd had plenty. And she wanted to get rid of every one. Rich pickings for Oxfam, but I didn't warm to the relish with which she cleared out his belongings. She said she never read books, only magazines. Not just the books themselves were to go but also the custom-made shelves on which they had stood. She wanted the space and was planning to have the entire building redecorated, inside and out. 'In colours *I* like!' she had said combatively.

I have a mental address book of various professionals – electricians, plumbers, decorators, plasterers, carpenters, roofers – whose phone numbers I know by heart and who I have called on for a good few SpaceWoman jobs. But there are some basic tasks I can do by myself. Particularly since I lost Oliver, I've had to turn my hand to many minor repairs at home. Now, when out working, my toolbox is permanently in the back of the Yeti. And dismantling the widow's late husband's shelves in the bungalow was not beyond my capabilities.

As soon as I saw the quality of the wood they were made of,

my first thought was of Dodge. Though much of his work uses cheap timber from pallets, he really appreciates the good stuff. I love watching him rub a hand along the grain of a fine plank. He seems to have an almost mystical association with the wood. Something pagan, perhaps. In fact, when I think about it, there's a lot that's pagan about Dodge . . . his lack of interest in commercial values, his instinctive empathy with the natural world.

I had texted him to say I'd be dropping by that afternoon, but I've no idea whether he got the text. Dodge possesses a mobile so ancient that its only smart skills allow him to make and receive calls. But how often he checks it – if ever – I'm never quite sure.

The presence of the van was promising. His 1951 Morris Commer CV9/40 Tipper, immaculately clean, as always. Dodge didn't believe that machines had a finite life. With proper maintenance, his van could go on forever. It was the same with the few power tools he used in his workshop. He had salvaged an electric drill from a skip, where it had been abandoned by a less patient owner and, without purchasing any replacement parts, had made it fully functional again. He derived great satisfaction from bringing condemned machinery back to life.

The workshop door was open, and I tapped on it to announce my presence. Dodge looked up from his workbench, as ever not meeting my eyes. I couldn't tell whether he was expecting me or not.

'Good afternoon, Ellen.' However many times I heard him speak, I still got an initial shock at his public school accent, so at odds with his scruffy exterior. I felt the same reaction when I remembered that his birth name was Gervaise.

'Hi, Dodge. Like I said in my message, I've got some wood for you.'

'That's great.' Again, he gave no indication as to whether he'd received my text. 'Would you like a nettle tea?'

'Please.'

I watched him make it, as I had many times before, on his ancient range, another item that someone had chucked out as being too old-fashioned, but which Dodge had refurbished. He always drank nettle tea. Foraging was very much part of Dodge's lifestyle. It was many years since he'd seen the inside of a supermarket.

'Have you heard from Ben?' he asked. He had a particular affection for my son. Without ever overtly talking about it, he seemed to intuit that the two of them suffered with mental health problems. And at one stage they even worked together, Ben bringing his artistic skills to painting some of Dodge's furniture. The relationship was good for both of them but couldn't have lasted. Dodge's desire to give away all his products sat uneasily with my son's acquisitiveness. Ben wasn't money-grubbing but, like his cartoonist father, believed in being properly paid for the exercise of his talents. That was part of the reason Ben had gone to America. Animators were much better paid over there.

'Not since you and I last spoke,' I said, trying to sound carefree about it.

'Mm.' Again, it was impossible to divine the thoughts behind that grunt. 'And Jools? Still working for you?'

'*With* me, I think might be more accurate. Increasingly, we're doing separate projects.'

'Good.' He poured the nettle tea into two battered but immaculately clean enamel mugs. 'Shall we take these and look at this wood?' And we ventured out into the freezing yard.

I got the reward I'd been hoping for when Dodge saw the deceased history teacher's shelving. Instinctively, his hands reached out to touch the planks. No, more than touch, it was a caress. I felt pleased. The last reminders of her late husband were out of the unsentimental widow's life and had found a home where they would be truly appreciated.

Just at that moment, it began to rain. Hard, heavy drops turning to hail as they spattered on the frozen ground.

'We must get the wood inside,' said Dodge. I couldn't really see why. A bit of rain or hail wasn't going to spoil it. But I didn't argue. Though they might not make sense to others, Dodge always had his reasons.

I'd spent a lot of time in Dodge's workshop, but I had rarely been inside the main house. I remembered, though, the tidiness with which everything was stowed there. Salvaged stuff tends to start off dusty and generate more dust in storage, but Dodge kept everything clean. It wasn't all wood. What must once have been the kitchen was piled high with scaffolding poles. A sitting room had been transformed by metal shelving into an ironmonger's store, with supplies of different sized hinges, letterboxes, door-knobs and other impedimenta, all stowed in labelled boxes.

Upstairs was where the wood was kept. Three bedrooms and what must once have been a bathroom. A glance at the contents revealed that there was some kind of quality control in operation. One room was full of cheap, splintery planks from deconstructed pallets. The next was pine and other soft woods. The biggest bedroom was heaped high with Victorian mahogany furniture at various stages of dismantling.

And in the fourth room, there were Dodge's most revered timbers, planks which he had selected for the beauty of their grain, shaped and sanded to perfection. These were the ones which he saved for special projects, commissioned furniture for public buildings. I congratulated myself on my discrimination, because that room was to be the destination for the shelves I had brought him.

But as we approached this shrine to superior timber, I could tell from Dodge's body language that something was wrong.

He looked into the room, looked around once again to be sure, and then said, 'Someone's been stealing my wood.'

FOUR

'Ellen, it's Theresa Carter.'

I was surprised by the call. I thought we'd come to the end of any dealings she might have with SpaceWoman. But all I said was, 'Good to hear you. I hope you're coping. It must be very tough.'

'Well, you'd know about that. You did say you're a widow, didn't you?'

'Yes. I did.' But I hadn't told her how closely the circumstances of Oliver's death mirrored those of her husband's. Or how much Humph's apparent suicide had stirred uncomfortable memories for me.

'I've been thinking a lot, Ellen,' said Theresa, 'about the weekend when Humph died.'

'I'm not surprised. It must have been a terrible shock.'

'Well, yes, of course.'

'Have you had further contact with the police?'

'Yes. They've been in touch. They tell me there'll have to be an inquest, but of course I'd worked that out for myself. They don't seem to think there'll be any difficulty about it. Straightforward case of suicide.'

'That's certainly the way it looks.'

'Ye–es.'

'You sound unsure.'

'I am. *Unsure* is, in fact, a very good word to describe how I feel.'

'Oh?'

'I wonder, Ellen, could you come over to Staddles to talk about it?'

'Sure. When?'

'Soon as possible. Today?'

'Yes. I could juggle a couple of work things around and come over.'

'Come for lunch.'

Theresa had called me early, before eight, apologizing for the hour, but I'm always an early riser, so it didn't matter. I made a couple of calls to reschedule my day's appointments. In my kind of work, it quite often happens that the care continues long after the actual job has been done. There are three or four housebound elderly people I first met because of a decluttering problem who I still try to see every week or so. Their social lives have become so restricted that, though a change of timing of my scheduled visit may cause disappointment, there's never a difficulty about rearranging. Loneliness is a cruel condition.

So, I changed my twelve noon promise to go and see Wanda Lyall to ten o'clock. Normally, I make midday appointments with her. Then, when I'm in her flat, I can casually open a packet of sandwiches, claiming I've brought them for my lunch, and make sure that she has one. Though Wanda looked remarkably fit for her age, I knew she wasn't eating enough. This wasn't a deliberate form of self-neglect. I think she just genuinely forgot to have meals. Which couldn't be good for her long-term health.

So, now it wasn't going to be at lunchtime, I would make sure I took a packet of Hobnobs with me for the rescheduled visit.

I was about to leave when Jools came downstairs. She'd been out the previous evening, and I hadn't seen her. She seemed to be going out more, which was good. I wanted her to have a social life. Aware of the danger of becoming a nosy mother in our cohabiting arrangement, I had not pried into what she was doing. I would wait, appropriately, for her to volunteer the information. And she hadn't volunteered anything much recently.

Jools was still working on student desqualoration in Worthing. Not on the same student house, another one. Wealthy parents, visiting the first shared house where Jools had worked her magic, told other wealthy parents about the tidiness of their offspring's accommodation. And a new income stream for SpaceWoman developed. It was all Jools's doing. I was struck by how well the work suited my daughter.

But I didn't dare think long-term. Again, in perhaps a rather cowardly way, I was waiting for Jools to say something. If she was going to stay in Chichester working for SpaceWoman, then changes would have to be made. I'd have to buy another car, for a start. She was currently travelling to and from Worthing by train, which wasn't ideal, given the amount of basic equipment a declutterer has to carry.

Whenever Jools and I met, the long-term future of her working with me was a second elephant in the room. The first elephant, of course, being what had happened in London to cause her breakdown. And that incorporated questions about what was happening to the Herne Hill flat. I wouldn't have thought there was any way Jools could afford to keep up the mortgage repayments on what I – or, rather, SpaceWoman – was paying her. Had she sublet the place? Was it about to be repossessed?

The two elephants were increasing in size at such a rate that there soon wouldn't be space in the room for them. I decided to initiate the long-avoided conversation.

'Would you like a coffee, Jools?'

'No, I'll pick one up when I get to Worthing.'

'Fine.' A silence. 'Jools . . .'

'What?' Not quite aggressive but moving in that direction.

'I just wanted to ask you about the flat.'

'What about it?'

'Have you got plans for what you're going to do about it?'

'What kind of plans?'

'Well, I mean, are you thinking of selling it or—?'

'I'm not going to sell it.'

'Oh. But how—?'

'It's all right. Just chill about it.' I'm sure she used the expression deliberately to annoy me.

'I'd just like to know—'

'It's sorted.' And, with that unhelpful remark, Jools set off for Worthing.

Compared to some of my other older clients, Wanda Lyall was quite self-sufficient. She had never been married and always lived on her own, for much of her life in the same flat with a sea front view in Bognor Regis. Since leaving secretarial college in her late teens, she had worked for the same local company which manufactured wheelchairs and other disability aids. She said often that she'd know where to go when she needed such assistance, but she remained mercifully mobile, thanks to many brisk walks along the promenade.

She'd retired at normal retirement age, which she thought was a blessing, 'because they were just bringing in computerized accounting systems and I couldn't be doing with that'. If she'd ever had a close emotional relationship with anyone, it wasn't something she'd mentioned to me.

Some might have regarded hers as a life of disappointments, but that wasn't how she saw it. Facing the indignities of age, she stayed remarkably chipper. Perhaps because her aspirations had never been high, she didn't feel unfulfilled.

Our paths had crossed for the first time when a male friend of hers called Bob had contacted me. He was worried about Wanda's accumulation of magazines. Most of her adult life, she had taken at least two weeklies and kept them all, 'because there are articles in them I like to go back to'. There were particular columnists, she explained, whose style she liked and whose writing she enjoyed rereading.

This habit, obviously, created a storage problem, of which Wanda, like many hoarders, was entirely unaware. But, when I entered the flat, for the first time, the sitting room and spare room were impassable, and the piles of magazines left only narrow passageways leading from the front door to her bedroom and the kitchen. The much-sought-after sea view could only be glimpsed by climbing on a chair and peering over the stacks.

Neighbour Bob came along on my first visit to introduce us. I'm always on my guard meeting a new client, but Wanda was neither aggressive nor demented. A small, very neatly dressed, birdlike woman, her marbles were all perfectly in place. She seemed, however, to see no incongruity in serving tea to us while we sat on chairs in her bedroom. She perched on the bed with the tray beside her, as if it was the most natural way in the world for a hostess to behave.

Bob lived in the flat directly beneath hers, and he had confided in me on the phone that he was worried about the weight of paper above bringing down his ceilings. He hadn't mentioned this anxiety directly to Wanda, just tentatively observing how little space she seemed to have in her flat. His comments had been greeted with blithe unconcern.

According to our prearranged plan, Bob had to go off on some errand, leaving me alone with Wanda. As agreed with him, I did raise his safety fears. Then occurred a phenomenon I have frequently encountered with hoarders – the moment of realiza-tion. Accumulating stuff is rather like living with someone for a long time. They age so gradually that you do not notice the changes until you suddenly see them one day, out of context, and ask yourself, 'Who is that elderly person over there?'

It was that kind of moment for Wanda. Her collection of magazines had built up so slowly, thin layer by thin layer, that she had not noticed how out of control it had become. But, after I had told her about Bob's fears, for the first time she saw the interior of her flat as an outsider might see it.

From that moment on, my task was relatively easy. Wanda immediately cottoned on to the fact that things needed sorting out. She was an intelligent woman.

Which was borne out by the titles she had collected. My expectation that they'd all be women's weekly magazines proved to be completely wrong. No, her reading of choice turned out to be *The Spectator*, *Punch* and *Private Eye*. I'm afraid I was enough of an intellectual snob to think better of her claim that they'd contain articles she'd 'like to go back to'.

By the time I left, on that first visit, Wanda Lyall and I were firm friends. I subsequently did some research and found that back copies of *The Spectator*, all the way from the magazine's founding in 1828, were available from its online archive. So, Wanda could 'go back to' any article from any issue without the necessity of having her own hard copy.

I also found out that, on the back pages of *Private Eye*, there were always small ads from completists trying to buy certain issues they were missing from the full set.

Wanda seemed reassured when I gave her this information, though I didn't believe that her attitude to computers had changed much since retirement had saved her from the new accounting software. I couldn't see her spending much time on the *Spectator* online archive. What my research had done, though, was to give her a face-saving reason for agreeing to dismantle her collection.

And, in fact, it turned out that she did make money from the sale of some treasured *Private Eyes*. I organized the transaction and its proceeds certainly covered what she paid for SpaceWoman's services. Which was very satisfactory all round.

Wanda and I also agreed on a new magazine retention rule. She remained an avid *Spectator* reader, but she agreed that she would only keep each new copy for four weeks. Then it went into the bin, so that the piles of past numbers did not start accumulating again.

And, under our agreement, she was allowed to keep a few back numbers whose contents or covers had particular resonance for her. She had a small pine chest in which she salted these away. I wasn't there to see which ones she selected but I got the impression that she knew exactly where in the teetering piles to find them. Her hoarding was not the work of a scatterbrain, but of an excessively organized mind. Which is quite often the case in my business.

When it actually came to clearing the flat, I did it at Wanda's pace. I'd keep my visits to about an hour, transferring pile after pile of magazines to the Yeti. Sometimes, a cover would alert some recollection in her. Given her reading matter – and her habit of having Radio 4 on most of the day – it was perhaps no surprise how well informed she was about politics. She also very definitely had her own views on public affairs. She was opinionated and witty.

Also, interested in other people. She always wanted to know how SpaceWoman was going, and I found her unjudgemental reactions a relief when I needed to unburden myself of some minor professional stress. Conversation with Wanda Lyall was always a delight. Which is probably why I was still seeing her regularly, a couple of years after the last excess magazine left her flat.

She was one of those defiant elderly women who would never admit under torture that she was lonely, but I think she appreciates my company.

That particular morning, when I visited her at ten after the call from Theresa Carter, we drank tea in the sitting room which, a couple of years previously, would have been totally inaccessible. Wanda was very aerated over a recent government policy statement, which had reversed earlier promises to protect the environment. The news had transformed her into a spitting bundle of fury.

Though the last of her own family, she felt a great responsibility for the safety of those who came after her and was articulate in her condemnation of governmental backsliding. Of course, when it came to the environment, she was talking my language. Though the primary aim of SpaceWoman is to help people, a declutterer, by definition, must have a green agenda.

So, we had a very vigorous discussion. Though we were both on the same side, the conversation flowed easily. I noticed with satisfaction that, without thinking about it, Wanda ate a couple of the Hobnobs I'd brought with me.

She then asked what I'd been up to with SpaceWoman. I mentioned that I'd taken on some work at Staddles, but then backed off. She hadn't heard of the place, and I really didn't want to get into a conversation about Humphrey Carter's death.

So, instead, I told her about a problem I'd been having with a couple in Barnham. The wife kept clearing her husband's accumulated rubbish from their garage and getting him to take it down to the recycling centre. He would set off in the car but, rather than dumping the stuff, he was stowing it away in another garage he was renting in Wick. Wanda was suitably amused.

When I checked my watch, I was surprised to see that it was after eleven. I had to go. I offered her the remaining Hobnobs to keep, but she refused to take them. Still, I had seen her eat a couple. Though I couldn't predict when she would next remember to have a meal.

While I was with Wanda, I'd heard the message ping from my mobile but didn't look at it until I was back in the Yeti. I checked who it was from. Fleur. My first instinct was to ignore it. Part of my mother's campaign to belittle what I did with SpaceWoman was to ring deliberately during what she knew to be working hours. A call in the morning usually meant an invitation to join her for a boozy lunch at the Goodwood. Though I always refused – and she knew I'd always refuse – that didn't stop her from continually making the suggestion. Our relationship was full of such oft-repeated square dances.

Yes, I should definitely ignore the message and go straight over to Staddles. But, as so often in dealings with Fleur, a sliver of guilt infiltrated my mind. Suppose she was genuinely ill … ? Suppose Kenneth had been given a terminal diagnosis . . .?

I listened to the message. Her voice was not that of someone unwell. It was bubbling with excitement. 'Ellen, ring me! I have the most thrilling news!'

My mother is one of those people who, having for a long time dismissed computer technology as a fad that wouldn't catch on, now embraces it with all the zeal of a religious convert. Much of her time at home, when not on the phone moaning at me or having long circuitous conversations with theatre friends about the good old days, she spends in front of her laptop.

She is on every available form of social media, considerably increasing the average age of the users on some of them. And she spends a lot of time on showbiz gossip sites. I have the rather sad conviction that she started doing that in the desperate hope of finding some reference to herself or her career. I can visualize her googling 'Fleur Bonnier' a lot. And being constantly disappointed by the modern world's lack of interest in her.

Sitting in the Yeti outside Wanda's, I gave in and pressed in the shortcut for her number.

'Ellen darling!'

'Hello, Fleur,' I said cautiously.

'Isn't it wonderful?'

'Isn't what wonderful?'

'You mean you haven't heard?'

'No,' I said patiently. I always get this when Fleur has some revelation to make.

'Well, it's the news about Ben.'

Had he been in touch with his grandmother before he'd been in touch with his mother? I was surprised how much the idea hurt.

'Have you had a call from him, Fleur? Or an email?'

'Oh no, I didn't hear the news directly from him.'

'Fleur, what are you talking about?'

'Do you ever read *Showbizzy Beez*?'

'No,' I replied flatly.

'Oh well, you should. All the absolutely up-to-the-minute goss is there!'

'Is it?'

'And there's something posted today about Ben.'

I couldn't believe what I was hearing. 'Ben? Ben Curtis? My son?'

'Of course Ben Curtis, your son. How many other Bens do you know?'

'Well, a few, but—'

'Anyway, according to *Showbizzy Beez*, Ben Curtis, your son, is only dating Layla Valdez!'

'Who?'

My instinct – the sensible instinct – was to restrain myself, wait until I got home from seeing Theresa Carter before I checked out Fleur's information on my laptop. I felt sure she must have somehow got the wrong end of the stick. I had never heard of Layla Valdez, but from what my mother said, she was the kind of showbiz character whom Ben wouldn't have touched with a bargepole. My son, like his father Oliver before him, didn't like razzmatazz. He favoured solitude over crowds.

But I was too curious to follow my instinct for restraint. I found *Showbizzy Beez* on my mobile.

And I read: 'After her very public split from Brad Forelli, Layla Valdez might have been expected to go to ground for a while to lick her wounds. But it looks like she's very quickly started licking something else. Only two days after her last sighting with Brad, Layla was seen getting very cozy in Santa Monica's exclusive Gazz Club with a new mystery beau. Mystery no longer, he turns out to be movie animator Benjamin Curtis. No time for post-split gloom for Layla. Looks like, from now on, her life is going to be a lot more animated!'

In the accompanying photo, Layla Valdez looked like a standard high maintenance Hollywood blonde.

But the man, around whose neck her arms were draped, was undoubtedly my son Ben.

FIVE

'Of course, there will be many more celebrations of this milestone in my life, but it's nice to get the whole juggernaut rolling with a small-scale domestic one. Contrary to appearances on certain occasions, I have always been at heart a family man.'

Theresa had sat me down with a substantial cup of very good coffee, facing the large screen in her late husband's study. I was watching the video their daughter Kirsty had taken on her phone at the birthday lunch. Theresa had left me to do so on my own, proposing that we eat after I'd watched it. Her manner did not suggest she was afraid that seeing the footage again might upset her. The suggestion seemed more that, on my own, I might be more objective in my viewing.

I wondered whether there was significance in the fact that Kirsty had taken the video rather than her sister. Chloe, after all, was the one who worked in television, so would be more familiar with filming technique, even at the simple level of a phone camera. On the other hand, she had on our brief meeting, expressed a cynical view of her father. Kirsty was his favourite, the chosen one.

'So, I am *enchanted*,' the recording went on, somehow investing the word with ambivalence, 'to be spending the actual day among my *nearest and dearest*.' Again, Humph's intonation seemed to be sending up the words.

And that was the tone in which he continued. 'Some people might feel it inappropriate on an occasion like this for the Birthday Boy to give his own toast but, the way I see it, the way I've always seen it, is: Follow the talent. Gathered round this table, we have people of enormous charm and varied skills but – let's face it – there's only one person here who's made a living – and had his talent for doing it recognized in numerous awards – by talking in public.'

I wondered how Chloe, another family member with a career

as a television presenter, reacted to that remark. But her sister's mobile phone camera was focused steadily on the main speaker. I could not gauge the thoughts of the others.

'Also, if I'm the one talking about myself . . . ' Humph chuckled '. . . I can avoid any element of criticism that might be voiced by others. And what might those criticisms be? From my wife Theresa, a woman for whom the term *long-suffering* could have been invented . . . what minor quirks of my character might, over the years, have caused her pique? Kirsty, may I suggest you turn your camera towards your mother while I consider this tough question.'

As if in answer to my unspoken plea, Theresa's face came into shot. She looked tolerant, used to her husband's dramatics, but also a little anxious, knowing him to be a loose cannon, capable of ruining social occasions on a whim.

But the words that followed were positively benign. 'All I know is that the list of my peccadillos is far too long for me to detail them now, and that I have been blessed to have the support of a beautiful wife who could overlook them all.' This was greeted by raucous shouts and a spattering of applause. Humph, however, could not leave the compliment unqualified. 'Well, the insignificant ones, anyway,' he added.

'Then we move on to my daughters. Was ever a man blessed with two such charmers? And what criticisms might two such paragons of pulchritude level at their Dear Old Dad? I wonder, Kirsty dear, could you shift the focus of your camera to your older sister?'

The pan across achieved, Chloe filled the screen, stunning to look at but antagonistic, ready to counter any barbs that her father sent her way.

Humph went on, 'Of course, we don't have to worry about the lovely Chloe being unused to the camera's gaze, do we? She is, after all, the doyenne of *daytime* television.' The emphasis he put on the penultimate word wasn't quite a sneer but moving in that direction. 'Following in father's footsteps . . . trying to achieve the same eminence in the media . . . and never quite succeeding.'

I could understand instantly why Chloe took such a cynical view of her father. On the video, a paroxysm of suppressed fury crossed her face. She seemed about to come back at him, but a glance to her left, towards her mother I assumed, stopped the words on her lips.

'And what might the lovely Chloe criticize me for? Having a more successful career than hers? Surely not. She is still young. Her career has not had time to develop yet. Who knows what triumphs lie in the future for her? Not in serious journalism, of course, but maybe some minor role in *Strictly Come Dancing* or *The Great British Bake Off* beckons for my oh-so talented daughter . . .?'

He let out a rueful chuckle. 'Of course, I'm only saying these horrible things about Chloe because I'm jealous of her. At her young age, I'd never even been in front of a camera. I was still a mere print journalist, a sad hack if you like. I genuinely believe that Chloe has a glittering career ahead of her.' Again, the humility was ambiguous. He had covered himself, without quite neutralizing the sting of his earlier remarks.

'What a pity,' he continued, 'that Chloe hasn't got a partner sitting beside her. He – or she – would, of course, have been welcome here, but they change so often, we didn't know which one to invite.'

The truce in hostilities had clearly been a brief one. Chloe's face once again contorted with rage, but another look at her mother silenced her.

'And, of course, having sons-in-law is not an unmixed blessing.' Kirsty's camera moved, anticipating what was to come, to frame a man I hadn't seen before. He could only be her husband, Garth Wickens. Pale blue eyes, long fair hair in an outmoded Mod style and a wispy beard. More than ever, I wanted to get a sight of his wife, who was holding the camera. To be able to see them as a couple. But that wasn't possible.

'Gaaarth . . .' Humph elongated the vowel in his customary mocking tone. 'Garth, where would we be without you? Well, we wouldn't have the prospect of a Booker Prize-winning novelist in the family, would we? Though we may have to wait a bit there. Old-fashioned as they are, the Booker Prize judges tend to go for writers who've actually had something published. Keep trying, Garth.

'No, but I'm being unfair. Once again I ask: "Where would

we be without you, Garth?" Well, we'd be short of two grandchildren, for a start.' An uneasy laugh around the table. 'Though
I'm sure, knowing how resourceful Kirsty is, she could have
sourced them elsewhere. Still, congratulations on ensnaring her,
Garth. A considerable achievement. And a man who has ensnared
Kirsty can regard that as the major achievement of his life. Surely
no one could expect him to do any more than that . . . and how
thoroughly Garth has taken that approach. The Beatles created
a "Nowhere Man". Garth has refined that concept and converted
himself into a "Nothing Man".'

The image shuddered as Kirsty, who was holding the phone,
laughed. Loudly. Too loudly. Uncomfortably loudly. Her husband
looked appropriately uncomfortable, but also cowed. This was
not the first time he'd felt the rough edge of his father-in-law's
tongue. But he knew that, on Humph's home territory, Humph's
rules had to be obeyed.

'And what criticisms might Garth have of me?' the Birthday
Boy demanded. 'Quite a few, I would think . . . including the
insulting words I have just spoken about him. But those words
were spoken in the spirit of a roast. And I'm not talking about
the pork roast we have all just enjoyed, cooked with Theresa's
customary finesse. No, I'm talking about a Celebrity Roast, an
American showbiz tradition in which a celebrity is roundly
insulted by his fellow artistes, but of course with great affection.
So that was what I was doing to you, Garth . . . and I hope you'll
take my words in the spirit in which they were meant, as part
of a Celebrity Roast.'

On the screen, the son-in-law grinned, to show what a good
sport he was, before Humph added, 'Except, of course, you could
never, by any stretch of the imagination, be described as a
Celebrity.'

More uneasy chuckling round the table. 'Next, the one person
present who could not really be defined as a family member, but
who is closer to me than any family.' The camera found another
figure I hadn't seen before. Probably about the same age as
Humphrey Carter, a grizzled face, corrugated hair, like wire wool
and a glaze in his eyes, perhaps from overindulgence at the
birthday lunch.

'Niall . . .' Humph supplied at least his first name for me. 'As you are all aware, I have known Niall as long as I have known Theresa, because she was at RADA with the woman who became Niall's wife, the lovely Zena. And, though all the appropriate things were said at her funeral, I would like once again to say how sad it is that she's not with us for this celebration. Zena was a brilliant actress – I refuse to say *actor* – and also a magnificent guest on *Humphrey Carter Interviews* . . . Zena was a woman who could, as I know well, add "something extra" to any day.

'And so, I welcome Niall, a man with whom I have shared so much.'

The man looked upset, and Kirsty tactfully moved the focus of the camera back to her father.

'I would like to say that, without Niall as producer, *Humphrey Carter Interviews* . . . would have been a complete disaster. I'd *like* to say that but, of course, it's not true. Without *me* as presenter, *Humphrey Carter Interviews* . . . would have been a complete disaster.' Humph chuckled bonhomously. 'Sorry, just joking there . . . as I'm sure Niall knows full well.'

As the camera was not on him, I could not know whether the producer agreed that it had just been a joke.

'What I haven't mentioned, of course, are the two youngest members of today's assembly.' Helpfully – and presumably with a degree of maternal pride, the camera found a boy of about eight and a girl of about six, dressed in their party finery. 'These are the ones who are going to carry the Carter name forward into posterity.'

'Not the *Carter* name, the *Wickens* name,' said an unseen voice.

'A mere technicality, Garth,' said Humph. 'They are undoubtedly our hopes for the future. Our only hopes for the future. And, if that's true, Gawd help us all!' The two children may not have fully understood his words, but they were already giggling. They worshipped their grandfather and enjoyed his little jokes.

'The trouble is,' he said, 'I can never remember their names.' The children giggled even more. This was a game they had played before. Humph struck his forehead in Mad Professor style. 'Oh yes, of course! I've remembered now. One is called *Botty* and the other is called *Potty*!'

The grandchildren had never heard anything so hilarious. As

he had shown throughout his television career, Humphrey Carter knew his audience.

'So, eighty years . . .' He also knew, from long experience, how to change his tempo and, with it, the mood of a room. Kirsty brought him back to the centre of her screen, almost in close-up. 'Ten more than the biblical recommendation of "three score and ten". No surprise, really, given advances in medical science.

'And I suppose my eighty years have featured some achievements. The family, obviously,' he said, as if he'd just that minute remembered them. 'And some level of renown in the public arena. Not all that I would have wished, of course. "Ah, but a man's reach should exceed his grasp, Or what's a heaven for?" I'm sure I don't need to tell any of you that that was written by Robert Browning.

'So . . . regrets?' He gestured to his wine glass and took on a drunkard's accent for the continuing quote from 'My Way'. '"I've had a few." What are they then, these regrets? I am slightly miffed that I never featured in the Honours List. But I think I offended too many politicians on *Humphrey Carter Interviews* . . . None of them have any sense of humour. Can't take a joke.

'And I think I could have been handed out a few more television awards, as well, but those juries are always loaded with people pushing their own stuff. And, again, they always go for the blandly uncontentious, rather than someone who's prepared to express their opinions. Something which, as you all know, I was never shy of doing.

'Glad to say my name features in the birthday listings for most of today's papers. Except the bloody *Guardian*. I'm far too right-wing for those lickspittle lefties, it goes without saying.

'Still, there'll be a revival of interest once they start the selected reruns of *Humphrey Carter Interviews* . . . on the box. Show the latest round of posturing adolescent stand-ups how a chat show *should* be done, eh?

'Then there's my memoir. Publishers still fighting over who's going to get the deal for that. When it comes out, there'll be a reassessment of my contribution to the arts. A very positive reassessment, it goes without saying.'

For the first time, a note of genuine bitterness crept into his voice as he went on, 'And I'm not sure that you lot ever appreciated quite how much I achieved. Still, "a prophet is not without honour, save in his own country, among his own relatives, and in his own house." Not Browning this time. Bloody King James Bible.

Finally impassioned, he said, 'I enjoyed being in the spotlight. I don't like being out of the spotlight!'

There was a silence while he regained control of himself. 'Anyway, when I'm gone, I'm sure I'll be appreciated more, get my rightful due. The obituaries will tell you what you missed. And who knows how soon those obituaries will be appearing?'

For a moment he seemed a little fazed by this reminder of mortality. But he was quickly back to his brash, loud self.

'So, now, a toast . . .' Humph topped up his glass from an expensive-looking bottle of Bordeaux. 'Will you please all raise your glasses in a toast to the person who has enabled you all to live in the very nice lifestyles you currently enjoy? And, in the secure knowledge that you'll miss me when I'm gone, the toast is . . . me!'

The double task of filming and raising a glass was apparently too difficult for Kirsty. The recording stopped abruptly.

SIX

'So, what did you think?' asked Theresa. We were eating a very good lunch of smoked trout with watercress and orange salad. I'd accepted the proffered glass of Pinot Grigio. I'd just have the one, I'm paranoid about losing my licence, which would effectively put an end to my SpaceWoman activities.

'You mean – do I think your husband sounded like a man intending to take his own life?'

'Yes. I suppose I do.'

'Well, to an outside observer, he might appear to be a confident man at the height of his powers, having fun at the expense of his family . . .'

'But . . .?' she prompted.

'But . . . I know how efficiently depressives can hide their real feelings, how they can appear to be the life and soul of the party, while actually in the depths of self-hatred.'

'You speak as if you're more than an *outside observer.*'

'Perhaps I am.' I decided to tell her. It wasn't information I'm in the habit of volunteering, but I thought it might be helpful to Theresa. 'My husband Oliver was a depressive. He committed suicide.'

'Ah. So, you know whereof you speak.'

'I'm afraid I do.' There was a silence.

To avert awkwardness, Theresa broke it. 'Well, that's just another reason why I'd appreciate your views on what happened. With you being a private investigator . . .'

'I'm not a private investigator,' I protested weakly.

'Well, you're someone with an acute understanding of human behaviour.'

That was a compliment I was prepared to take.

'Have you had anything definite from the police?' I asked.

She shrugged her elegant shoulders. I was struck again by what a beautiful woman. Theresa Carter was. In their seventies, few can get away with sleeveless. Arms and hands are great betrayers of age. But she looked stunning in a grey linen shift. The magnificent cheekbones were emphasized by the minimum of expert make-up.

Not for the first time, I wondered what it must be like to grow up as a beauty. I mean, I've been found attractive by sufficient men who I wanted to find me attractive, but I knew I'd never be in Theresa's league. I recalled that a friend of mine called Hilary had found her exceptional looks brought as many drawbacks as benefits.

'Obviously there'll have to be an inquest,' Theresa replied. 'But the police don't seem too worried about the outcome of that. There was enough evidence for them to think a suicide verdict probable. Humph had been prescribed temazepam for a bout of insomnia some years back and he'd never taken it off his list of repeat prescriptions. So, he was effectively stockpiling them.'

'Planning for what happened at the weekend?'

Another shrug from Theresa. 'Possible to read it that way. It's how the police seem to read it, anyway. Or maybe that's just the impression they want to give me. Maybe they're actually involved in some elaborate double bluff, allaying my suspicions while they search for proof that I or one of my family killed Humph.'

'Presumably they've checked all the logistical stuff, who was in the house, that sort of thing?'

'They did most of that right at the beginning. I told them Kirsty, Garth and the kids went on the Sunday evening. Chloe and Niall stayed over.'

'When did Niall go? He wasn't here when I arrived on the Monday morning.'

'No, he'd woken early and gone back to The Hayes – that's his house.'

'Did you see him when he left?'

'Only briefly, just to say goodbye.'

I was thoughtful for a moment. 'Did the police tell you anything else . . . about the reasons they thought it was suicide?'

'The magazine article seemed to be the clincher for them. Did you read it, Ellen?'

'Yes.'

'Anyway, the police didn't share much of their thinking with me, but they reckoned the perpetrator leaving a note made it much more likely to be a suicide.'

'Rather than what?'

'Presumably, an accidental overdose. Or foul play?'

'Hm.' I was glad I'd photographed the article when I was last in Humph's study. I'd have a closer look at it when I got back home. 'The views your husband expressed in that article, were they things you had heard him say before?'

A rueful grin. 'Humph had views on everything. He was a talker. He hated silence, liked to be surrounded by people. That's why he liked working in television. Television people hunt in packs. Nothing he liked better than being in the centre of a group and talking. Always talking. And, if there were only two in the group – him and his wife – that didn't stop him from talking.

'So, yes, I have heard him express the views which appear in that article, the recommendation that everyone should be quietly eliminated at the age of eighty.'

'Then, surely—?'

'Wait, Ellen. I have also, on many occasions, heard Humph argue the exact opposite. That human life should be extended infinitely, that there's always time for one more adventure, one more glass of fine wine.

'He was a controversialist. He loved expressing opinions which he knew would annoy people. Some of them he believed in, some of them he believed in at the moment he expressed them, some of them he never believed in. Humph was a man who needed constantly to be *heard*.'

'Sounds quite tiring.'

'That is a very good word for it, Ellen. Oh, I loved Humph, but I did find living with him very *tiring*.'

'And do you remember when he wrote the article, the one that could have been his suicide note?'

Theresa shook her head. 'No. I probably read the piece when it was published. I can't honestly remember. Humph rarely showed me his journalism before he filed it. That wasn't him being secretive, just it was part of his professional, rather than his domestic life. It was the same with his public appearances and after-dinner stuff. I was very rarely there. He knew I'd heard it all before.'

She offered me coffee. I accepted.

Then, when Theresa had put on the machine, she said, 'So, I come back to my original question . . .'

'Do I think your husband sounded like a man intending to commit suicide?'

'Exactly.'

'I didn't know him, Theresa. It's hard to make a judgement about someone I don't know. The more interesting question to me is: Do *you* think he sounded like a man intending to commit suicide?'

'No,' said Theresa Carter. 'I don't think he did.'

I had a lot to mull over as I drove back in the Yeti from Staddles. Theresa's words had added fire to a small doubt which had been flickering in my mind since the moment I discovered Humph's body. The suicide set-up had somehow always seemed too pat, too contrived, too staged. The note in the form of a printed magazine article. Perfect for the police, what they are always looking for – an open-and-shut case.

But, if it wasn't suicide . . . The chances of an accidental overdose were slim. Humph was quite capable of drinking too much Famous Grouse and, if he was worried about insomnia, he might resort to some of his stockpiled sleeping tablets. But surely not in the quantity that could kill him? Also, he'd have taken them orally, washed down with whisky, not crushed up in the bottle.

There was really only one other solution that offered itself.

Theresa had said she'd email me a copy of Kirsty's video which I would watch again on the laptop when I got home. I'm sure it contained clues I'd missed in what I was thinking of increasingly as a murder investigation.

Before I got back to Chichester, I had a phone call. I'm set up to answer them in the car, but only do if it's one of the kids. If it's work, I return the call when I'm parked up or back home. On this one, the screen flashed up 'Theresa' while I was driving. So, I answered it.

'Sorry, Ellen, something I forget to mention while you were here . . .'

'Oh yes?'

'Niall . . . Niall Fitzpatrick . . . Humph's former producer who you just saw on the video . . . '

'Mm?'

'Well, as you gathered, his wife Zena – my dear friend – died . . . not that long ago. And he's stuck on his own, in a big house, and he's undecided whether he wants to move . . . and the place is becoming something of a tip and . . .'

I knew where this was leading. It was a speech I had heard many times before.

'Anyway,' Theresa went on, 'I was talking to him about what you had done – and what you were proposing to do – here at Staddles, and I said maybe Niall could use your services . . .'

'Sounds good.'

'So, Ellen, do you mind if I give him your contact details?'

'Of course not, Theresa. In common with most people running their own businesses, I rarely turn down work.'

But that wasn't the only reason I was pleased by the suggestion. Niall Fitzpatrick had known and worked with Humphrey Carter for a long time. He might have insights on the mystery of the man's death.

The next day, Dodge picked me up in the Commer van. I had a client in Cocking, an artist who'd been forced by arthritis to abandon his brushes. He also used to give talks on painting, when he turned his studio into a lecture hall. He was having to give that up, too, and wanted me to find a good home for thirty folding chairs. When I'd casually mentioned this to Dodge, he'd said he knew a place in Portsmouth that was crying out for chairs.

Which was where we were driving that morning.

He was silent on the way there and I respected his privacy by saying nothing either. My mind was still full of the Humphrey Carter mystery.

Dodge hadn't told me our destination. When he parked outside a nondescript empty shopfront, he didn't volunteer anything about what the place was, and he refused my offer to help carry the stuff. Clearly, I was to stay in the van.

Dodge went inside, not carrying anything, and emerged soon

after with a couple of scruffy-looking young men who proceeded to unload the chairs. Two minutes later he was back in the cab, restarting the engine.

I didn't ask, but it was evident that his helpers knew him, and I reckoned the place was the drug rehabilitation centre where Dodge volunteered. He had never openly talked to me about the work he did there, but I somehow intuited it. And the knowledge increased my belief that drugs were involved in his major break-down and subsequent change of lifestyle.

I was prepared to have a silent return journey if that's the way he wanted to play it, but he actually initiated conversation. 'You know that wood . . .?' he said.

'The shelving I brought you?'

'I wasn't thinking of that so much as the wood that got stolen.'

'Yes. I remember.'

'The person who did it . . .'

'Hm?'

'. . . really knew what they were looking for.'

'So you said at the time.'

'Which is strange. How did they know it was there? How did they know I loved wood?'

'Maybe it was someone you'd met?' I didn't want to suggest it might have been one of the addicts from the place we'd just visited. 'Someone to whom you'd mentioned that you love wood.'

'I've never mentioned to anyone that I love wood.' It was almost a reprimand.

'Then I have no other suggestions,' I said.

'It intrigues me,' said Dodge mysteriously. 'I'm going to find out who it is.'

When the Commer van dropped me back at home, I did as I'd intended and watched the birthday lunch video again. Now that my vague suspicion had been strengthened by Theresa's views, I looked at it with different insight.

And my main conclusion was that Humphrey Carter was far too fond of the sound of his own voice to deliberately silence it forever.

I opened up a Word document on the laptop and was writing notes about the video when my mobile rang. Jools.

'Hi, Mum.'

'Hi. How're you doing?' She must be nearly finished on the latest Worthing student house.

As she confirmed. 'Pretty well there.'

'Good.'

'Thing is . . . '

'Yes?'

'People in the house are suggesting having a party to celebrate the end of the decluttering.'

'Great idea. And something that, I'm sorry to say, has never happened at the end of a job I've done. Presumably, they're having the party with a view to ensuring that the place'll need decluttering again tomorrow?'

My daughter chuckled. 'No. I've given them very firm instructions that they have to tidy everything up afterwards.'

'Excellent. You're a credit to SpaceWoman.'

'Thing is . . .' Jools said again.

'Yes?' I said again.

'They've invited me to stay for the party.'

'I think you definitely should. It is your work they're celebrating, after all.'

'That's true. Anyway, I was thinking . . . likely to be late . . . there will be drinking involved . . . Might make more sense if I were to stay over in the house, get a train back in the morning.'

'Good idea.'

'Fine.' Jools sounded relieved. What had she thought – that I was going to forbid her to stay out overnight in Worthing? My daughter was well into her twenties. 'OK then, Mum. I've got a bit of final tidying to do. See you tomorrow.'

'Sure.' A moment of mother and daughter harmony. Which I then proceeded to destroy by saying, 'Oh, and remember, we do need to have a proper talk soon about the Herne Hill flat.'

'I told you,' she snapped. 'It's all in hand.'

Why did I always fall into that kind of trap? The fear that I might be turning into my own mother, Fleur, suddenly attacked me. Surely not. Yes, my daughter and I were capable of rubbing each other up the wrong way, but surely our relationship was different? I wasn't as selfish as Fleur. Was I?

It took a cup of coffee for me to put that thought to the back of my mind and regain my equilibrium. And, when I had regained it, another, more appealing, thought came into my mind.

Did Jools's recent evenings out and her wish to stay overnight in the house mean there was someone in Worthing she was attracted to?

I would really love my daughter to be in a relationship with someone.

'Ellen darling . . . ' Fleur on the phone. All I needed.

You keep hearing of these women who adore their mothers and want to spend every minute of the day on the phone to them. Well, they're very fortunate, but it's not an experience I can claim to have shared. I'm not sure I've ever received a call from Fleur which I wouldn't have preferred to leave for the answering machine.

But, as usual, I had answered this one. I managed to get in a 'Hello.'

'Kenneth's had his results,' she said, channelling Lady Macbeth.

'So, what are they?' I asked, yet again allowing her to dictate the course of her narrative. For which I kicked myself. Yet again.

'Oh, they say they can't find anything.'

'Well, that's good news, isn't it?'

'Huh. What do doctors know?' A characteristic Fleur response.

'But, if they can't find anything wrong with him . . .'

'Ellen, if they didn't think there was anything wrong with him, why did they want him to have the tests?'

This was very familiar. And very exasperating. I replied curtly, 'They wanted him to have the tests to *prove* there was nothing wrong with him.'

'But they haven't proved that there's nothing wrong with him. It just means they haven't *found* what is wrong with him.'

'Well, Fleur, what do *you* think's wrong with him?'

'I don't know. I'm not a doctor, am I?'

Through gritted teeth, I asked, 'Does Kenneth think there's something wrong with him?'

'It's always hard to tell with Kenneth.'

'Is he complaining of any pain?'

'Kenneth doesn't complain.'

'Then it sounds like you have nothing to worry about.'

'But it doesn't stop me worrying, Ellen. Kenneth might just be putting on a brave face.'

I couldn't take much more of this circuitous conversation. 'Fleur, I'm afraid I do have to get on and—'

She cut in. 'Have you heard anything from Ben and his new girlfriend?'

'No.'

'I thought not,' said my mother darkly.

SEVEN

It was strange. Jools hadn't been back living in the house for long, but I was still aware of her absence when I woke the next morning.

And that, of course, made me think of Ben, with whom I'd spent more time cohabiting in recent years. But I didn't want to think about him. He had a new girlfriend.

I wouldn't be human not to have wanted to know more about Layla Valdez. Feeling slightly grubby as I did so, I went back on to *Showbizzy Beez* in search of further information. From there, I was redirected to various other showbiz websites.

It turned out that Layla was actually English by birth, born in Liverpool. In her teens she had been talent-spotted and featured in a couple of British television series I'd never heard of. This had led to her going to the States to star in a couple of Netflix series I'd never heard of. She had millions of followers on Twitter and Instagram (neither of which I was on).

The Brad Forelli, from whom she had recently split, was a high-profile basketball player with the Los Angeles Lakers. Their very public break-up was chronicled. And again, it was confirmed that Layla was currently dating the 'Brit animation whizz, Benjamin Curtis.'

I should have been more unambiguously pleased. I really wasn't one of those mothers who thought no woman was good enough for my precious son. I genuinely did want Ben to make his own way in life. I'd encouraged him to go to the States. I wanted his experience to be as broad as possible. And, if Layla Valdez was the right person for him – hooray!

But I knew the ways of girlfriends. They either cosied up to the loved one's mother to get her onside. Or they subtly – oh, so subtly – insinuated to the boyfriend that he was too close to his mother and wouldn't really be able to assert his own identity and have a meaningful adult relationship until he put some distance between them.

From Ben's telephone silence, I reckoned Layla might be the second kind. Which, of course, I could accept. I could accept anything that made Ben happy.

But all I could think about was my son's terrible vulnerability, the mental illness he'd inherited from his father. The illness that had proved so devastating to Oliver. I was terrified of history repeating itself with Ben.

I tried to think of Jools, instead. With her, I had at times worried whether she had all her social life online, whether she ever actually engaged with people in real life. If she was getting some kind of relationship going with someone in Worthing, then that was unadulterated good news.

My mobile rang. It wasn't a number I recognized.

'Hello? Is that SpaceWoman?'

'Yes.'

'Ellen Curtis?'

'Yes.'

'My name's Niall Fitzpatrick. I'm a friend of Humph and Theresa Carter.'

'Yes, I know exactly who you are. Theresa mentioned you when I saw her recently.'

'Oh, good. And did she say I might be in touch?'

'She did. I gather it's a decluttering problem . . .?'

'You could say that. You could also describe it as "total chaos". Since my wife died . . .'

'Yes, Theresa told me. I'm sorry for your loss.' Sounded stilted, but sometimes only a formal cliché fits the circumstances.

'Thank you.' There was a pause when he might have been about to say more about his late wife but decided against it. Instead, he went on, 'I was wondering whether you could come out to my place to assess the scale of the damage . . .?'

Serendipitous, when an investigation moves ahead under its own momentum.

The Hayes was a detached house on the foothills of the South Downs near Amberley. It was large, but not as large as Staddles. I wondered if that was a metaphor for Niall Fitzpatrick's relation-ship with Humphrey Carter. It would fit with the way the producer had been patronized in the birthday lunch video. An entire career of always being measured against Humph's success. And always coming up short.

Niall must have been looking out for me, because I had only just parked the Yeti on the gravel driveway (less imposing than the wide sweep in front of Staddles), when he appeared from the front door.

He shook me by the hand. 'Such a pleasure to meet you.'

Because he'd been sitting down in the recording I'd seen, I hadn't realized how short he was. Also, while Humph had expanded outwards as he grew older, Niall seemed to have dried up, become wizened, with very little flesh between skin and skeleton. But he was still a good-looking man.

I remembered that he'd been at RADA with Theresa and Zena Fitzpatrick, whom he'd married. Which would put them all probably round the same age. Early seventies, nearly a decade younger than Humph.

Niall had an appealing ruefulness about him. This was intensified when he welcomed me into the house. He gestured to the cluttered hall and said, 'You see my problem.'

I did. I also instantly recognized the kind of problem it was, one I'd seen quite often in cases of bereavement. The surviving partner was just not practised in the business of running a house. Niall Fitzpatrick hadn't developed the instinct to 'tidy up after himself'. As a result, the hall was littered with old newspapers, coats abandoned on the floor rather than hung up, emptied Amazon delivery boxes. It looked like student chaos. I wondered whether I should enlist the help of Jools, SpaceWoman's newly appointed specialist in that area.

Incidentally, I had also come across that kind of chaos in a household where the deceased was the husband rather than the wife. It wasn't just a gender thing. The shock of a partner's death can take many forms, and just not noticing, or not doing anything about the build-up of mess, is quite a common one. In the new loneliness of a life designed for two, there seemed no point in maintaining basic tidiness just for one.

And, if the deceased had been particularly house-proud, reaction against their standards was almost a statement of grief.

I shared Niall's ruefulness in the grin with which I greeted his remark, and ventured, 'I don't think I'd be wrong in expecting the kitchen to be rather worse.'

'You're a very perceptive woman, Ellen.'

He led me through. Yes, my prediction had been correct. All the signs of enforced bachelordom. Dirty dishes in the sink, empty pizza boxes, opened tins. And a lot of bottles. Mostly wine, but quite a few whisky as well. Famous Grouse, I noticed. Imitation once again being the sincerest form of flattery?

'I'd offer you a cup of coffee but . . .' He looked around the wreckage of the kitchen and shrugged.

'I'd like a cup of coffee,' I said, quite deliberately. 'And, if it's going to be easier for me to make it . . .'

He looked quite attracted by the idea for a moment, but then reminded himself of his duties as a host. 'No, I'll do it. Only instant, I'm afraid.'

'That's fine.' I found a chair that had nothing piled on top of it and sat down.

There was evidence of Zena everywhere I looked. I'd noticed photographs in the hall, and her face looked out from the kitchen walls too. Familiar. I'd seen her so many times on television that I felt I knew her. And yet, confronted by her image, I realized I knew nothing about her. Partly, it was the staged nature of the photographs. Somebody with her profile would constantly have been in promotional photoshoots, but even the family pictures, Zena with her husband and two boys, did not have the untidy spontaneity of most people's family records.

None of the photos I could see went back as far as their student days but, when Niall first met her at RADA, Zena must have been absolutely stunning. As must Theresa.

'How long is it,' I asked, 'since your wife died?' I always use the words 'die' and 'death'. I prefer them to the euphemisms.

'God,' he said, 'I want to say six months, but it's longer than that. Seven months, maybe.'

'And do you see your children a lot?'

'Hardly at all. Both boys, having watched their parents twitching through the trauma of show business, trained as accountants. Both work in banks, one in Singapore, the other in Sydney.'

'Ah.'

'Obviously, they were back here for the funeral, but . . . They send odd texts and stuff to assure me they're still alive. That generation don't seem particularly good at keeping in touch.'

I felt a pang as I thought of Ben. 'And have you got other close family?'

Niall shook his head. 'I was an only child.'

'Ah.'

'You were asking, Ellen, I assume, whether there was some angel of mercy, like a sister, who could fly in and sort me out.'

'It was a thought.'

'No. The only ministering angel currently on my radar is you.'

It wasn't said flirtatiously, but I could still see that, in spite of his age, he had a boyish charm that might appeal to some women. Not me, by the way. I seem to be impervious to desire for men these days. My only mild skirmish with another man since Oliver's death had not ended well.

Niall continued, 'Theresa recommended you. She said you were doing great stuff at Staddles.'

'Well, I'd hardly started there. Very much work-in-progress.'

'She described you as "comforting and sympathetic".' Again, the charm was there in the compliment.

'I try to be,' I said. 'Anyway, what is it you need doing here?'

The slump of his shoulders encompassed the whole mess. 'You can see what needs doing.'

'No, I asked what *you* needed doing.'

'Ah. Good distinction.'

'Because I can tidy things up for you. A cleaner could tidy things up for you. But, within a couple of weeks, it would all once again look exactly as it does now. You know and I know, Niall, that, for real change to happen, you're going to have to change your mindset.'

'I was rather afraid you'd say that.' He looked glum.

'I'm not saying it's going to be easy. As someone who's just walked into this house, I can see it's still full of Zena. For you, that must be unimaginably more the case. But, for me to be able to change things, you'll also have to make some changes.'

'I know.'

'You don't have to change your feelings for the one you've

lost, but you do have to start looking to the future as well as the past.'

Niall looked at me with a sardonic grin. 'You've done this before, haven't you?'

'Yes,' I admitted. 'A good few times.' It was on occasions like this that I felt grateful for the Cognitive Behavioural Therapy course I'd taken.

'Hm.'

'And it's completely understandable how, at the moment, you feel incapable of making any decisions, but life has to go on.'

'Does it?' he asked despairingly. Then, feeling he needed to backtrack. 'Sorry, that sounds overdramatic. Of course life has to go on . . . for other people.'

'And for you.'

'Mm.' A silence, then he said, 'Theresa told me you were a very reassuring presence.'

'I'll take that as a compliment.'

'So, you should. I gather you were advising her on what to clear out with a view to their downsizing.'

'Yes. But whether that's still her plan . . . Like you, she's not in a good place for making big decisions at the moment.'

'I'd think, with Humph gone, she'd want to downsize more than ever.'

'Possibly. But I'm sure she hasn't had time to think about that yet.'

'Probably not.'

'What about you, Niall? You're six, seven months ahead of Theresa in the mourning process. Have you thought about moving?'

'Only in the vaguest way. I'm sure I must. This place is far too big for one miserable old git. Trouble is, that's the kind of thing I would have discussed with Zena. And then she'd be the one who actually made the decision.'

'I see.' Time for practicalities. 'Listen, Niall. I think I – in other words, SpaceWoman – can help you get out of this chaos but, as I said, I'm going to need a lot of input from you.'

'Yes, I thought you might.' Rueful again.

'I'm not questioning the shock and unhappiness you're feeling in the wake of Zena's death. It's something that'll never go away completely.'

'Oh yes. Theresa said you were a widow.'

'That's right.' I moved briskly on. Not the time to go into the details of Oliver's death. 'Niall, I'm not going to delude you into believing your life will ever be the same, but I can perhaps help you to see a way forward to a different way of living.'

'I'd be grateful for that,' he said humbly.

'What I suggest is that I take a look at the rest of the house, either on my own or with you giving me a guided tour . . .'

'Go on your own. I don't want to be shamed by my own mess.'

'Fine.' I drank down the last of my coffee. 'I'll start straight away, and when I come back down we can work out an action plan.'

'Sounds good to me.' I stood up but, before I could leave the kitchen, Niall asked, 'Has Theresa talked to you about her theory of Humph's death?'

'The idea that it might not have been suicide?'

'Exactly that.'

'She did mention it, yes. What's your view?'

'I think it's complete nonsense. I don't think she's thinking straight.'

'Crazed by grief?'

'Something like that. Unable to accept the idea that Humph wanted to end it all.'

'Just for a moment going along with Theresa's theory, the person who wanted to kill him must have got into his study and put the ground-up sleeping pills into the bottle of Famous Grouse.'

'Yes. And how likely is that to have happened?'

'Presumably, everyone in the family knew about Humph's drinking habits?'

'Yes. Well, possibly not the grandchildren, but everyone else.'

'And he didn't lock his study, did he?'

'God, no. He loved people wandering in and out. And on the Sunday morning the grandchildren had organized a Birthday Treasure Hunt, so everyone had been chasing all over the house.'

'Logistically at least then, someone could have got into the study and adulterated his whisky?'

'Logistically, maybe, Ellen. But Theresa's in a world of her own, having these strange notions. That's part of the bereavement process. I tell, you I've had some pretty crazy ideas about Zena since she . . . since she . . .' He couldn't say the word. 'Still do get them occasionally.'

'Hm.' I needed to establish some basic facts. 'On the eightieth birthday weekend, Niall, when did you leave Staddles?'

He looked at me with a sudden grin. 'Oh, I'm being lined up as a suspect now, am I?'

'No. I'm just trying to piece together the sequence of events . . . to find out where Theresa's getting her crazy notions from.' That was, at least partly, true. 'Did you leave on the Sunday?'

'God, no. Just as well, with the amount of alcohol I had inside me. It's always going to be a heavy session, when I'm trying to keep up with Humph.'

Trying to keep up with Humph – it could be an encapsulation of Niall's relationship with his friend. But I kept the thought to myself.

'Anyway, I woke up about five on the Monday morning, in that dreadful dehydrated, headachy, pukey state you get with a hangover . . .?'

'I remember,' I said wryly.

'Well, I knew I wasn't going to get any more sleep, so I thought the best thing I could do was come straight back here.'

I curbed my nannying instinct and didn't ask whether he'd thought he was safe to drive so soon after the previous day's skinful.

'And did you see Theresa before you left?'

'No. Didn't want to wake her.'

I nodded, as if in appreciation of his thoughtfulness. 'Did she tell you she'd shown me the video of the birthday lunch?'

'Yes, she did.'

'On that, Humph certainly didn't come across a man preparing to end it all. But then I know how skilled people can be at disguising their true feelings. And someone like him, used to being in the public eye, I'm sure he was an expert at it.'

'He very definitely was.'

'But, come on, Niall. I hardly met Humph. You've known him for decades. Your opinion of his state of mind is much more valuable than mine.'

'OK.' He paused to gather his thoughts. 'Well, Humph was definitely a man who liked making the grand gesture. He had a sense of drama, particularly about himself. So, I guess his suicide might be in character in that sense.'

'The person I saw in that birthday lunch video seemed to have boundless self-esteem.'

'I agree. That's how he always came across. But having spent so much time with him, I know he did have dark moments too.'

'Did he talk of suicide at those times?'

'Oh yes, of course he did. He was a bit of a drama queen. He liked saying things to shock people. So, announcing that he was about to top himself was entirely in character.'

'But did you ever believe him?'

'No, I thought it was just Humph being Humph. That is, until the events of his birthday weekend.'

'Hm. And the article, the magazine article that seemed to have been used as a suicide note . . . did you know about that?'

'I'm sure I read it at the time. Humph was proud of his journalism and, as ever, he wanted an audience. I'm sure he read out stuff he'd just written to anyone who'd listen. Theresa and the girls must have got an earful over the years. I know he'd often run his pieces by me.'

'With a view to you making editorial suggestions?'

'Good God, no. With a view to me saying how wonderful they were.'

'Ah.'

'Humph didn't like criticism. That's why he stopped doing social media. But he still needed praise to endorse his self-validation.'

'Hm. You know your psychobabble jargon, don't you, Niall.'

'Thank you. We aim to please.'

'Going back to Humph's dark moods . . . were there real-life events that triggered them? Or did they just suddenly appear?' I was trying to work out whether Humph had actually been a congenital depressive.

'Oh, there were triggers. He reacted badly if things didn't go the way he wanted – particularly in his professional life. He hated bad reviews, hated any kind of rejection.'

'So, presumably, he wasn't happy when *Humphrey Carter Interviews . . .* was pulled from the schedules?'

'That's an understatement, Ellen. He was absolutely furious. But that was the thing with Humph. Some people, when they suffer a setback, turn their anger inwards. Humph always expressed it.'

'How? I mean, how did he express it when the show was cancelled?'

'By bawling out the bosses of the production company and the schedulers. And bawling out everyone he met, actually.'

'I noticed from the video that he had a good line in diminishing people.'

That evinced a very heartfelt 'Yes'.

'You sound like you've suffered from the rough side of his tongue.'

'More times than I can count.'

'But you still regarded him as a friend?'

'Oh God, yes. I mean, under the stress of live television, a lot of unwitting insults are thrown about, but all that's soon forgotten in the bar afterwards. Come on, I've known Humph for nearly fifty years. I'd be a real glutton for punishment if I kept seeing him all that time and didn't regard him as a friend.'

I wondered. Maybe Niall Fitzpatrick was a bit of a 'glutton for punishment'. I've known other instances of weaker individuals being in thrall to a dominant personality who constantly diminishes them.

I changed tack. 'In the video, Humph seemed to be complaining that insufficient fuss was being made about his big birthday. I mean, public fuss, in the media, that kind of thing.'

'That was another reflection of the size of his ego. Humph never thought enough fuss was made about him. Back in the day, when his picture and opinions were all over the newspapers, it still wasn't enough. He still felt he was underappreciated, and other celebrities were getting more coverage than he was.'

'But presumably he was pleased to know they were going to rerun some of the *Humphrey Carter Interviews . . .* shows?'

'Ah,' said Niall in a way that suggested there was an issue about the subject.

'He mentioned those were coming up at the birthday lunch.'

'Yes, Ellen, I know he did. He was lying.'

'Oh?'

'There had been plans for a selective rerun of some of the best ones. Like his interviews with John Smith when he was Labour leader, and Robin Cook. Some of the showbiz ones, too . . . Sammy Davis Junior, Jerry Lewis. Humph hustled like mad with his contacts in television to get them to agree. And for quite a while it looked like it was going to happen.

'But then it got all the way up the management to the broadcaster, the guy who actually gives the yeah or nay, and he gave it a resounding nay. As I recall, the killer email said, "Who knows or cares who Sammy Davis Junior and Jerry Lewis were? Come to that, who knows or cares who John Smith and Robin Cook were?"'

'With, I guess, the implied question: "Who knows or cares who Humphrey Carter was?"'

'Spot on, Ellen. But Humph had bigged up those reruns so much, told so many people about them – not just friends and family. He'd posted lots of stuff about it on social media before he cut himself off from that stuff. He'd talked about them in every interview he was asked to do. So, he couldn't announce they weren't happening without a terrible loss of face. He couldn't admit to himself that they'd been pulled. That's why he mentioned them at the birthday lunch.'

I was thoughtful. 'Might Humph have thought they were more likely to do the reruns if he was dead? As a kind of tribute to his career?'

'So, he topped himself in the hope that the reruns would happen?' Niall suggested.

'That might be a motive for suicide.'

'A rather fanciful one, Ellen,' he said wryly. 'And not guaranteed to have the desired effect. I doubt if the broadcaster would be keener to repeat interviews by a dead Humphrey Carter than he would by a live one.'

'OK. At the lunch Humph also mentioned a memoir that publishers were "fighting over".'

A sardonic grin from Niall. 'I'm afraid that didn't look likely to happen, either. No, so far as the media were concerned, Humphrey Carter was very definitely "yesterday's man".'

'He would have hated realizing that.'

'Certainly would. He just couldn't come to terms with the fact that the world had forgotten about him. And that, in my view, is the reason why Humph committed suicide.'

I nodded thoughtfully. Niall seemed uncertain whether to say more. Then he decided he would. 'There was another reason, too.'

'Oh?'

'Everyone knows that work always came first with Humph, but he could also be hurt at a personal level.'

'People with large egos are often hypersensitive.'

'Yes. Certainly true of him. Petulantly upset by any tiny reverse in his life. That's why, like I said, he suddenly cut himself off from social media – didn't like people posting nasty stuff about him. And he wasn't good at processing negative feelings. He could do anger, but that was really the extent of his emotional repertoire. So, a major bereavement . . . he wouldn't be able to deal with it. He'd shut it all in, have no release for his emotions.'

'Are you saying that Humph had had a major bereavement?'

'Yes.'

'What – a family member? A brother or . . .?'

'No.'

'So, whose death was it that might have proved so dramatic for him?'

'Zena's.'

EIGHT

'I knew virtually from when it started,' said Niall.

'Oh?'

'Zena and I got married while we were still at RADA. Too young, of course. Some people say everybody marries too young. Zena went straight into big tellies and the West End. My acting career was less successful. Probably took me longer than it should have done to realize my talents lay on the directing and producing side.

'Anyway, Zena took a couple of years off to have the boys, then went straight back into work. She was in demand, never wasn't in demand. By then, Theresa, her great mate from RADA, had married Humph and they had the two girls, round the same time we had the boys. We spent a lot of time together, the four of us with the four kids. Holidays together, that kind of thing.

'Then my career took me off for long stints directing in regional theatres, while Zena's was less theatre and more telly, most of it London-based. Anyway, I came back from three months doing a *Cherry Orchard* at Salisbury Playhouse and Zena announced to me that she had started an affair with Humph. He was still a journalist back then. He'd interviewed her for some colour supplement and, as they say, one thing had led to another.

'Zena was very clear-headed about it. She knew Humph would never leave Theresa and the girls and, anyway, she had no desire to move in with him. But she told me straight that she wanted the affair to continue. My options were either to move out and start divorce proceedings . . . or live with it.

'I said I'd live with it.'

He looked at me for signs of shock or pity. Or disgust, possibly? I gave none, so he went on, 'I had no desire to find someone else. I loved Zena. I wanted to be with her for the rest of my life.'

He gave me another look to check my reaction. I remained tactically impassive. I didn't want him to stop. But I was surprised by the bluntness of what he said next.

'I've never had a strong libido. Sex was pleasant enough, but I didn't have a burning urge to be having it all the time. Zena was different from me in that respect. And, in a way, taking the onus of the sex away, our marriage was better than ever.'

He looked around at the chaos of his kitchen. 'That's why I'm such a mess now Zena's not here.'

Time for me to put in a question. 'I can see that from your point of view. But was Theresa as ready to accept the situation?'

'She didn't know about it.'

'Oh, come on . . . You're talking about something that went on for thirty years or more. She must have known.'

'I swear she didn't. Still doesn't. That was part of my deal with Zena. She made me promise I would never tell Theresa.'

'But she was living with Humph. There must've been lots of unexplained absences and . . .'

'He was always up and down to London for meetings. He and Theresa have a flat in Covent Garden.'

'He can't have met Zena there. Surely, Niall, when Theresa was in the flat, she must have noticed some signs of someone else having been there.'

'Humph and Zena didn't meet at the flat. Anonymous London hotels.'

'But they were both famous faces. The paparazzi must have been on to them?'

Niall shrugged. 'Seems not. I don't know whether they disguised themselves or . . . don't know.'

I wondered. I suppose it was possible. The wife, as they always say, is the last to know. And I had come across comparable instances in my SpaceWoman work.

'So, what you're saying Niall is that the loss of Zena is another reason for Humph to have taken his own life?'

'She was an amazing woman,' he said bleakly. 'Look at the effect her death has had on me.'

Jools was there when I got home. I heard her coming down the stairs just after I'd got to the kitchen. She wasn't wearing her SpaceWoman livery of blue polo shirt and leggings, but a well-cut denim dress I hadn't seen before. Maybe it had been a freebie from her days in the London fashion world. She looked tousled, as if my opening the front door had woken her up. She also looked relaxed and pleased with herself. I hoped that meant things were going well in Worthing.

'Hi, Mum,' she said. 'Student houses done. Wondering what you required of me next . . .?'

'There've been a couple of enquiries on the website. Maybe you'd like to pick up on them.'

'OK, I'll check them out on my laptop.' She moved as if to return upstairs.

I suddenly saw an opportunity. 'Just have a cup of coffee first.'

'Why?' she asked.

'Don't you want a cup of coffee?'

'I'm happy to have a cup of coffee,' she said cautiously, 'but I'm sure you've got a reason for suggesting it.'

'Well, maybe . . .'

As I turned to the coffee machine, my daughter sat at the kitchen table with an air of resignation. 'What is it?'

I made and poured the coffee in silence. Then I sat down opposite her. The expression on her face was one I remembered from childhood. The pout that came out when she thought she had been told off unfairly.

'It's about the flat.'

'Oh, you keep going on about that.'

'I know I do. But it's because I want some information about it.'

'Why?'

'Because something strange happened to you up there and you've never told me what it was.'

'Mum, can't you accept that there are areas of my life which I don't want to share with you?'

'Yes, I can accept that. But when it's something that concerns your health and wellbeing . . .'

'Look at me.' She spread her hands wide. 'Do I look ill?'

'You look great.'

'Good. I feel great too.'

'I'm delighted to hear it.'

'So, Mum, what are you worried about?'

'I am worried because when you were last in the flat, you

hadn't eaten for days and you were in the middle of a major breakdown.'

'I was a bit upset.'

'That doesn't cover it, Jools. And you know it doesn't.'

'God, you're getting so like Fleur.'

That was a low blow. I ignored it. 'I'm not probing into your private life. I'm just concerned about practical things.'

'Like what?'

'Like who's paying the mortgage on the flat.'

'I've got it covered.'

'What does that mean?'

'It means that the mortgage is being paid. It's not in arrears. And the monthly payments to you for what you lent me for the deposit, you'll be getting those too.'

'But how, Jools?'

She stood up. 'I'm going to check those SpaceWoman enquiries.'

'Well, if you want to use the Yeti to go and see one of them this afternoon, that's fine. I've got accounts and invoices to do.'

'Thanks. I'll see what's come up.'

I couldn't stand it. I stood up and barred her exit from the kitchen. 'I'm sorry, Jools. But you have to tell me – how is the mortgage being paid?'

'Does that matter?'

'It does to me. From what you told me, you hadn't been earning anything from your online fashion stuff for some months. So, back then, how was the mortgage being paid?'

'Well, it's obvious.'

'Not to me it isn't.'

'Someone else was paying it.'

'Who?'

'The guy in the flat above.'

Before I had time to put my amazement into words, my daughter had swept past me and gone upstairs to her bedroom.

Shortly after, I heard the sound of her footsteps coming quickly down the stairs. I just had time to register that she was in her SpaceWoman uniform before the front door slammed and I heard the Yeti starting up.

*   *   *

'Ellen, have you been checking out *Showbizzy Beez*?'

'No, Fleur,' I said wearily. 'Of course I haven't.'

'Oh well, you should have done. That is, if you're mildly interested in what your son is getting up to.'

I didn't respond to the dig, just asked, 'What's happened?'

'Well, you know he and Layla Valdez are an item?'

'Yes, Fleur.'

'I thought you might have forgotten. You showed so little interest when I first mentioned it.'

'I hadn't forgotten,' I said evenly. I was practised in gritted teeth responses to my mother.

'Well, it's all been going very well. They've been spotted together at many of LA's hottest nightspots.'

'Good for them.'

'But what's exciting is that Layla's first feature film is about to be released.'

'Ah.'

'Made by Warner Brothers. It's the real deal. Will have a theatrical release before it's streamed.' I could always tell when Fleur was quoting something she'd read. 'But the big thing is, Ellen darling . . .'

'Yes?' I prompted, familiar with her theatrical pauses.

'The theatrical opening is going to be in London. Odeon Leicester Square.'

'Ah.'

'A glitzy showbiz première.' I didn't feel the need to react. 'And, what's more, according to *Showbizzy Beez*, Layla Valdez is going to be there . . .'

'Oh, good.'

'. . . accompanied by her new beau, Benjamin Curtis.'

'Ah.'

'I'm surprised he hasn't told you about it, Ellen.'

My mother has always known how to hurt.

NINE

Worrying about Jools is a relatively recent preoccupation of mine. I always thought Ben was the flaky one and she was the stable one. Only gradually am I realizing how much she too was affected by Oliver's suicide.

And now there was a new spectre to haunt my thoughts of her. 'The guy in the flat above.' Who was he? Undoubtedly an older man. Having lost her father in her early teens, Jools might well be susceptible to the charms of an older man.

What form any such relationship might take worried me deeply.

Though I'm punctilious about keeping proper accounts for SpaceWoman – I know too many cases of small businesses coming unstuck over inaccurate records – I'm much more lax about my personal finances. Statements become available online every month and I rarely look at them. Unless I'm adding a direct debit or changing a standing order, I assume everything's in hand. I know the bank will alert me if there's a danger of going into the red. And there never is.

That makes me sound awfully Goody Two-Shoes, but my caution was born of living for so many years with Oliver. Though enviably disciplined about meeting deadlines for his cartoons, his business paperwork was a complete shambles. Sometimes I was tempted to accuse him of using the 'I'm an artist, so I can't be expected to deal with the mundane details of life' excuse, but I don't think that would have been fair. His mind just wasn't good at engaging with practicalities. Forms terrified him. He was afraid of filling them in incorrectly and reaping disproportionate official retribution.

I came to believe that, like so many things, it was a symptom of his depression, a constant fear of being in the wrong. It was the same with booking holidays. He just couldn't do it. He did actually once talk about that. He said, 'Suppose I book somewhere and when I get there, I'm depressed? Then it'd be my fault.'

Anyway, the result of all this was that I took over management of both Oliver's business finances and the family ones. And, though I didn't have a natural bent for that kind of thing, I went through all the boring small print and made myself be good at it.

Hoping to find out more after my unsettling conversation with Jools, I logged on to my personal bank account and checked the regular monthly payments I received from her, reimbursing me for the deposit on the Herne Hill flat.

I started with my most recent transactions. What I found there astonished me. With growing incredulity, I went back through earlier statements. The same pattern recurred.

The payments had been made regularly, without a break. But the last one that had come out of Jools's bank account was nearly a year before.

Since then, I had been receiving money from 'P. Driscoll'.

Whoever he, she or it might be.

I read the papers. I listen to the radio and watch television news. I'm fairly aware of what's going on in the world.

And I've heard of what is called a new phenomenon in the realm of property (though I suspect it's been going on, under another name, for a very long time).

It's called 'sex for rent'.

'Hello. It's Theresa.'

'Oh, hi.'

''I heard from Niall. Gather you've been to see him.'

'Yes.'

'Do you think you can help with all that chaos he's generated?'

'Do my best. As with most of the cases I deal with, the basic problem's in his head. The state his house is in is just a symptom.'

'Yes. He's taken Zena's death really badly.'

'So it seems.' I hesitated before pursuing the subject. 'They were very close?'

'Oh yes. I mean, obviously they had long separations because of their work commitments, but Humph and I were amazed by the way they always bounced back together like they'd never been apart. It was a very strong marriage.'

There was something almost repellent about the idea of Humph discussing with his wife the marriage of the woman he'd been having a long-term affair with. But, obviously, I didn't comment.

'Well, Ellen, it'll be great if you can help Niall get his life back together.'

I didn't think a grief-struck widower's need for SpaceWoman's services was the main reason for Theresa's call. And so it proved. 'I wonder, did Niall say anything about Humph's death?'

'He mentioned it, obviously. I mean, he could hardly have avoided mentioning it, given the fact that it was you who recommended me to him.'

'True. And what do you think his view was . . . you know, given the doubts that I told you about?'

'Niall seemed pretty convinced it was suicide.'

'The obvious explanation. The police's explanation. And, I gather, what is likely to be the coroner's explanation, when we get to that point.'

'Any more information on that, incidentally, Theresa? Date of inquest, date of funeral, and so on?'

'No. It's very unsettling. They can't release the body for the funeral until after the inquest, and there seems to be some delay over getting that fixed. Don't know why. I've asked lots of official-type people and they don't seem to know either.'

I thought this might be a significant development. If it was taking the police so long to gather evidence for the coroner, then perhaps they didn't think the death was as straightforward as it had first appeared.

I said, 'There hasn't been much in the press about Humph's death, has there?'

'No. he would be very pissed off about the lack of coverage.'

'And I haven't seen any suggestion that the death might have been suicide.'

'No, thank goodness. His television agent is handling the press. He's very good at it. Not the first time he's had to withhold information about one of his clients. People like that are as much a PR company as an agency these days. Have to do a lot of damage limitation over their clients' misdemeanours. As a result, they're good at controlling the information that goes to the press. Mind you, when we get the inquest's verdict, it'll all have to go public.'

'How're you bearing up,' I had to ask, 'under the strain?'

'I'm all right,' came the stoical reply.

'Have you thought about what kind of funeral you'll arrange?'

'Just a small family cremation as soon as we get the go-ahead. Then I suppose I'll try to organize a memorial service in London. St Bride's probably – that's often called "the Journalists' Church"'. But I'm not sure how many people would come. So many of Humph's former colleagues are no longer with us. Oh well, I'll face that problem when it arrives.'

As she had been in all my dealings with her since her husband's death, Theresa Carter remained practical and unemotional. How she behaved when she was on her own, realizing the magnitude of change in her circumstances, intrigued me. But I didn't know her well enough to be able to guess at that.

'Incidentally, Theresa,' I asked, 'have you had further thoughts about what we discussed on the phone . . . you know, about the idea that Humph's death wasn't suicide?'

'Yes. I haven't changed my mind. In fact, the more I think about it, the more convinced I become that either it was an accident—'

'Pretty unlikely, given the way the sleeping pills were ground up into the whisky.'

'You're right. So, really, we're only left with one explanation.'

'Yes. Have you mentioned your suspicions to the police?'

'Good God, no. I haven't got nearly enough evidence to make the allegation stick. Besides . . .' She hesitated.

'Besides . . . what?'

'Well . . . I don't like the thought of making accusations against members of my own family.'

'I can fully understand that.' I pressed on, 'If it was a family member, have you considered who was most likely?'

'I can't go down that route, Ellen. It's too upsetting.'

'Hm. Look, are you sure you want me to go on investigating? If it's upsetting you . . .?' The offer was, I suppose, genuine but I'd have been disappointed if she'd taken me up on it. I was getting far too caught up in the case, to leave it at that juncture.

'No, no. Please, Ellen. I want anything that can be found out to be found out.'

'Very well.' I did a quick assessment of how much of what Niall had confided I could pass on. Made my decision. 'You know the reruns of his interviews that Humph talked about at the lunch . . .?'

'Yes, I know they weren't going to happen.'

'Ah. Niall told me that. I didn't know that you—'

'Humph had told me. Swore me to secrecy, though. Didn't want to make the admission in front of the family. And I know the memoir wasn't likely to happen, either.'

'Really?' I seized the possibility of more potential evidence. 'Had he actually started writing the memoir?'

'No. Though he had gone to the length of getting some old diaries out to check background stuff.'

I pounced on a potential source of evidence. 'Had he kept a daily diary for a long time?'

'No, Ellen. It wasn't that sort of diary. Not one to record every thought that crossed the radar of his sensitive soul. Humph would never have written anything like that. These were engagement diaries, chronicling not what he had done but what he was going to do. Quite useful to him to jog his memory for people and events.'

'And is it all clear to you, what's written in the diaries?'

'What do you mean?'

'You can understand it all?'

'It's not very difficult, Ellen. Mostly names of restaurants and the people he was going to meet there.'

'No entries that don't make sense? Secret codes?'

'Nothing as melodramatic as that, no. A few initials and things I couldn't identify. Nothing important. Humph knew a hell of a lot of people.'

'Hm. Had he got as far as making any notes for the memoir?'

'No. He was very grumpy about the whole business. He'd thought his literary agent had only to float the idea of a memoir from Humphrey Carter to find publishers falling over themselves to offer him a contract. He certainly wouldn't have written anything on spec. It was a kind of arrogance with him. "I've made it a principle, throughout my professional life, never to write anything that hasn't been commissioned."' Though it wasn't exactly an impersonation, Theresa had captured her late husband's tone of voice perfectly.

'But, sadly, Ellen, his literary agent wasn't finding it as easy to get that commission as Humph had hoped. The one publisher who expressed mild interest wanted an outline first. Humph was furious about that. "What do they think I am – a first-time writer? I've never had to submit an outline for a book before!" His agent told him that the world of publishing was changing, that a lot of his established authors were being asked to submit outlines.

'What the agent didn't say – but what Humph undoubtedly understood – was that the publisher was doubtful as to whether anyone was interested in the life of Humphrey Carter. Asking for the outline was just playing for time before the proposal was rejected.'

'Hm,' I said. 'So, he had that on top of the decision not to rerun the interviews. Presumably both disappointments would have hit him pretty hard?'

'Undoubtedly. But it was always difficult to tell with Humph how deeply he was hurt by things. There was so much bluster and ranting and blaming everyone else. It was like the fact that he'd never been given an honour. He regarded that as part of an establishment conspiracy against him. He saw other broadcasters getting OBEs, CBEs, even knighthoods, but he was passed over every time. I suggested that this might possibly be because he'd expressed some fairly trenchant republican views in his journalism and on television, but he couldn't see it. He thought he was being unfairly victimized. Humph could be very paranoid at times.'

Theresa sighed. 'Even having lived with him for so long, I never really knew what went on at the centre of his being.'

'It can't have been easy, living with an outsize ego like that.'

'I got used to it. Actually, it was part of his attraction. Also, Humph could be very funny. Silly, even. Not a lot of people saw that side of him. No one has ever made me laugh as much as Humph did.' For a moment, there was a catch in her voice, quickly covered up. 'Mind you, he could be bloody infuriating, too.'

'Faithful?' I dared to ask.

'Not technically,' she replied with surprising candour. 'The odd cub reporter in his journalism days. Researchers when he got into television. It hurt me the first few times. I'd still rather it hadn't happened. But it did, he was that kind of man. His ego always needed massaging.'

'How did you find out about them, the other women?'

'Humph wasn't very subtle. Took them to our London flat in Covent Garden, where . . . what shall I say? I found evidence.'

It sounded to me like he'd wanted his wife to find that evidence, evidence of short encounters with unremembered younger women. With the one who mattered, Zena, he had gone for the anonymity of hotels.

'Initially,' Theresa went on, 'my discoveries led to big rows. But then I just accepted it. And there's been much less activity in that area in recent years.' She was admitting inadvertently – or perhaps deliberately – that the sexual component had ceased to be part of their marriage. I wondered how long before it had ceased to be a part of his relationship with Zena.

'None of his affairs were long-term, just flings. I soon came to realize that he wasn't doing anything that threatened the long-term stability of our marriage.'

Again, a slight catch in the voice. But it seemed that Niall's assessment had been correct. Theresa Carter had never known about her husband's liaison, lasting more than thirty years, with her best friend.

There was no way round it. I knew that, as soon as Jools returned, we were going to have to have a confrontation.

I had expected her to rush upstairs to her bedroom but she joined me in the kitchen, quite meekly. After all, she had SpaceWoman business to report on.

'So, was it anything promising?' I asked. 'The people you went to see?'

'I think it could be. Young couple moving into her mother's house. The mother, who's very fit for her age, is moving into an existing annexe which they've always referred to as the "Granny flat". All seems harmonious at the moment. The mother isn't being forced into it. The whole thing was her idea. And, obviously, she's helping them out. Given the current price of property, they'll be getting a much bigger place that they could afford in the usual way. A win-win situation.'

I waited for the 'but'. I knew there'd be one.

'But,' said Jools, 'the trouble is that the main house is full of furniture and décor which isn't exactly what the young couple would have chosen for themselves. The mother keeps saying that she wants them to feel free to do whatever they want to do with the place. It's their home now, after all.'

I anticipated another 'but'.

'But,' said Jools, 'every time they suggest actually making a change, removing a large piece of furniture, repapering the walls . . . the mother comes up with some sentimental reason why they shouldn't do it. "That desk was bought by your late father when he retired. It's one of the few things of his I've got left." You know the kind of stuff.'

'I certainly do.' I had had to deal with many comparable situations in my SpaceWoman work. And, of course, living with Fleur had been a master class in the various forms of emotional blackmail. 'So, Jools, how've you left it?'

'The mother's away, visiting a friend, at the moment. That's why they were happy for me to go to the house. Which was good, because I had a chance to look round and see the scale of the problem. They're going to come back to me with a time when I can meet all three of them.'

Even a few weeks before, I might have suggested that I should also be present at that encounter. But Jools had shown such aptitude for the SpaceWoman work that the thought hardly crossed my mind. Though it did bring with it the recurrent question of how long our collaboration would continue. Which, of course, raised more issues, like buying another company car, getting Jools into a position where she had some stake in SpaceWoman rather than just receiving a salary. But it wasn't the moment to go into any of that.

'Excellent,' I said. 'It's great to have you around to deal with younger clients. I'm sure they understand your language better than mine.'

Jools grimaced. It was partly a grin, but it had an element of wariness in it. She knew I was about to raise another subject.

Which, of course, I was. 'Jools,' I said, trying not to sound wheedling, 'I really do need to know what's happening about the flat.'

'I told you. it's all fully paid up. Nothing to worry about.'

'All right, it's fully paid up. But it's not being paid up by you or me. It's being paid up by *P. Driscoll.*'

'Oh, congratulations on your research,' she said snidely. 'You got his name.'

'But who is he?'

'I told you. He's the guy in the flat above.'

'But why is he paying for everything?'

'Because he offered to. I was in a bit of a bad way. He could see that, and he offered to pay the mortgage, so that at least I didn't have to worry about that.'

'And he offered to pay the instalments on what I'd lent you as well, did he?'

'Yes. Don't look at me like that, Mum. What would anyone else do in the circumstances? I'm not going to . . . what's that expression involving horses?'

'"Look a gift horse in the mouth"?'

'That's the one. Well, I wasn't going to do that, was I?'

'No. But what was your deal with him?'

'There wasn't any bloody deal!' shouted my exasperated daughter. 'Oh, there's no point in talking to you!' And, with that, she rushed upstairs.

Leaving her mother even more bewildered.

TEN

'Hi. It's Chloe Carter.'
'Good morning.'
'Is that Ellen Curtis?'
'Yes.'

'I have to ring this time of day, obviously, because of the show.'

'Right.' I thought it possibly characteristic of her that she'd assume I'd know which show she was talking about. I'd got the impression she'd inherited something of her father's ego. Also, when I came to think about it, the mention of the show was entirely gratuitous. You don't need an explanation for ringing someone at eleven o'clock on a Monday morning.

Not that I was impressed by the reference, anyway. I never watch daytime television. I waited to hear the reason for her call.

'I've just been on the phone to my mother.'

'Oh yes?'

'And it seems she's been talking to you about Humph's death.'

'She has.'

'So, no doubt she's told you her theory that he was murdered?'

'She did mention it, yes.'

My words prompted an exasperated sigh from the other end of the phone. 'That's typical of Mum at the moment. I'm afraid she's losing it a bit.'

'I didn't get that impression when I last saw her.'

'No, she hides it well. All that RADA training makes it easy to present a false front to the world. But I'm afraid the marbles are rather rattling.'

I wasn't convinced, but all I said was, 'You know her better than I do.'

Chloe's 'Yes' was heavy with world-weariness. 'Listen, Ellen, I'm worried about Mum spreading this kind of rumour around. I think we're currently safe from the media till the inquest happens, but we don't want the waters muddied before then.'

'And you reckon, if Theresa's allegations of murder got around, they would muddy the waters?'

'Of course they would. It'd be a nightmare. All over the press and social media. Total disaster.'

'So, Chloe, you've never thought there was anything odd about your father's death?'

'Depends how you define *odd*. Suicide, by definition, is, at the very least, unusual. And desperately sad.' She seemed to add that as a sentimental afterthought. I could envisage the heart-rending look she would address to the camera as she said it on live television.

'Anyway,' she went on, 'Mum seems to take your opinion very seriously.'

'Does she?' It was something I hadn't thought of.

'Yes, seems to think you're some kind of genius private investigator. So, I'm begging you to try to persuade her to stop spreading this stupid idea about murder.'

'Can I ask why you are so convinced it was suicide?'

'Oh my God, so many reasons. Look I'm sorry, I have to go in a minute. But I'd love to talk to you at length about this. Are you ever up in London?'

'Yes. From time to time.'

'Well, if there'd be any chance of us meeting up . . .?'

'I'm sure there would be.'

A plan was beginning to form in my head. A plan that might help sort out two of my problems at the same time.

'It's happened again.'

'What's happened again?'

It was unusual for Dodge to be ringing me. Usually, I'd be the one making contact.

'More wood stolen.'

'From the store in your house?'

'That's it. And, again, it's the best stuff that's been taken.'

'So, what are you thinking of doing about it? Not contacting the police?'

'God, no!' Something in his past made Dodge very unwilling to have any dealings with the police. 'No, I was planning maybe some kind of ambush to catch whoever it is next time they break in.'

'Worth trying,' I said.

'You see, I get the feeling they're watching me.'

This was slightly worrying. Dodge's mental health was fragile. Was this the start of a paranoid episode?

He went on, 'They seem to know exactly when I've finished preparing the best wood and that's when they take it.'

'By "preparing the best wood" you mean getting the nails out, sanding it down, that kind of stuff?'

'Exactly.'

'And where do you normally do that? In the house?'

'No. If it's raining, I do it in the workshop. Otherwise, in the yard.'

'Outside? That must be pretty cold this time of year.'

'It's fine,' he said gruffly.

'So, when you're working in the yard, you reckon you could be being observed by someone hiding in the woods?'

'That's what I'm thinking, Ellen.'

'Hm. It must be unnerving, feeling you're under surveillance.'

'A bit,' he said. 'More . . . intriguing, though.'

'Mm.'

'Anyway, Ellen, I was thinking . . .'

'What?'

'If I'm going to catch this mysterious thief . . .'

'Yes?'

'I might need some help. You see, I reckon they've worked out that, if the Commer van's parked outside, then I'm on the premises. So, they drive in when they know I'm away.'

'Makes sense.'

'Well, I was thinking, next time I prepare some of the best wood . . . which somehow the thief will know about, I drive away in the Commer. The thief thinks I'm off the premises and drives in . . . but in fact I'm round the corner in another car so that I can follow them.'

'And might this other car,' I asked, 'be a blue Yeti with a SpaceWoman logo on the back?'

'Ideally, yes.'

I will never fully understand how Dodge's mind works.

'What're you doing lunchtime next Thursday?'

It was Fleur. I prepared my usual response. She knows full well that I put in a working week for SpaceWoman, but she keeps on trying to drag me out for boozy lunches with her at the Goodwood Health Spa Café.

But before I could get the familiar formula of words out, she went on, 'Because I'm having lunch in London with Benjamin.'

'Benjamin? Are you talking about my son Ben?' To say I was shocked would be an understatement.

'Of course your son Ben! Though, actually, he's calling himself Benjamin now.'

'Fleur,' I asked patiently, 'what's going on here?'

'Nothing's going on here, Ellen. I just contacted my grandson because I knew he was going to be in London next week, and he was kind enough to invite me to join him for lunch on Thursday.'

I was so taken aback that I literally could not speak. Fleur went on. 'Of course, I chose the right time to ring because of the time difference. I knew about all that from when I was fielding constant calls from Hollywood.'

To call them 'constant' was a bit strong. I remembered the time well. I was in my teens. A Hollywood producer (though not one anybody seemed to have heard of) saw Fleur in a West End play that he raved about. He said she'd be perfect for a part in the next movie he was setting up. Must have been school holidays because I remember how much Fleur went on about it. I also remember mildly wondering what, if any, arrangements she'd make for my care if she was spirited off to 'L.A.', as she kept calling it.

So, there were a couple of phone calls after he went back to the States. Then, in the manner of Hollywood producers who nobody'd heard of, he vanished off the face of the earth. The movie never got made.

'How did you contact Ben?' I asked.

'I rang him on his mobile phone,' Fleur replied patiently, as if to a child. 'Something you could easily have done, Ellen,' she added reprovingly. 'But he said he hadn't heard from you for a long time.'

'I've texted him.'

'A text, Ellen, is not the same as a proper phone call.' Another rap over the knuckles for me. And an example of my mother's idiosyncratic views on social protocol. 'Anyway, as I told you – though you didn't seem very interested – Benjamin's girlfriend Layla's movie is premiering next Wednesday at the Odeon Leicester Square.'

'Yes, I remember.'

'The movie's called *Virgins of the Fall.*'

'Is it?'

'Warner Brothers,' she said in awestruck tones, before going on, 'And I thought . . . well, if Benjamin's going to be in London, it'd be nice for me to see him . . . even if you don't want to see him.'

That did make me crack. 'It's not that I don't want to see him! I've just been waiting for him to contact me.'

'Well, often one just has to swallow one's pride and make the first move . . . in a family conflict.'

'Fleur, this is not a family conflict!'

'I don't know what else it is. Anyway, don't worry, Ellen. I've smoothed things over. And I've asked Benjamin and Layla . . . when I see them for lunch on Thursday . . . will it be all right if I bring you along too?'

The fact that I have got so far through my life without murdering my mother is a constant source of amazement to me.

ELEVEN

There had been a time when Fleur had had a better line of contact to Jools than I had. They had indulged in a kind of simpering girl talk which I had found – as they intended I should – infuriating. But then my relationship with my daughter had never been as close as the one I had with my son.

But now . . . for me to be making arrangements with Ben, using Fleur as an intermediary . . . It hurt more than I had ever imagined. Checking the time difference, I rang his mobile.

The message played. He's always been good with accents and now he was doing stoned Californian. 'Hi, this is Benjamin. Clearly I'm not here, though whether that means I'm actually absent or on my own private planet, I leave you to guess. But, if you want to be in with a chance of me getting back to you, you'd better leave a message.'

It was slick, it was glib, but it wasn't my son. No, worse than that, it was my son, but my son on one of his manic highs. And, from spending so long with his father, I knew exactly what followed those manic highs.

I had thought quite a lot about the message I should leave. I wanted to sound affectionate and practical. I did not want to sound as if there was the smallest hint of emotional blackmail in my words. Having been brought up by Fleur, I am an expert on the subject of emotional blackmail.

All I said was: 'Hello, Ben, it's your Ma. Very glad to hear from Fleur that we'll be seeing you on Thursday. Give me a call if you have a moment. Lots of love.'

I had a text back later that afternoon. 'See ya. Fleur's got the gen. Love ya.'

That was not the kind of thing Ben normally wrote.

I felt myself losing my son.

And I wasn't exactly getting closer to my daughter. Jools flashed through the house later in the afternoon, just to change out of her SpaceWoman gear. She said she was meeting 'some people' in Worthing. And she might well 'crash down at someone's' overnight.

I didn't raise the issue of the Herne Hill flat again. I knew I wasn't going to get any more out of her about that.

Which made me even more determined to follow through my plan.

With the prospect of meeting Chloe in mind, I thought I should perhaps have a look at her oh-so-important television show. So, after a bit of channel-hopping on the Tuesday morning, I managed to find it.

Chloe Carter was co-hosting with a floppy-haired youth, whose tones were firmly Geordie. (Television executives were again trying to appeal to the widest possible demographic. Male and female, received pronunciation and a regional accent. I thought it was a surprise, in the current climate, that neither of the presenters was a person of colour.)

And I'd been right, when I spoke to Chloe on the phone, in imagining her soulful looks to the camera. It wasn't a hard news show. World events were wrapped up in one-minute bulletins on the hour and half-hour. The rest of the programme featured what are described by the ghastly phrase 'human interest stories'. It was all reunions with lost pets, babies' first words and pensioners unable to pay their heating bills. The predominant tone was 'mateyness', broken up by commercials for nappies and stairlifts. Necessities for the beginnings and endings of lives. Not my kind of fare at all.

But there was no denying that Chloe was good at what she did. She had inherited her father's natural poise in front of the camera. And, having seen how tough and abrasive she could be in real life, I was impressed by the image of caring concern she managed to project.

Chloe Carter was a professional and the camera loved her.

I had intended to pay another quick visit to Wanda Lyall, but time defeated me, so I had to make do with a phone call. I could tell from her voice that she was disappointed not to be seeing me. But she gave assurances that all was fine. She was sticking

to our mutually agreed rules. In the flat, only recent issues of
The Spectator and *Private Eye* were visible. She had been
checking through some of her old favourite magazines for the
columnists she liked rereading, but obediently replacing them in
their pine chest when she'd finished.

Wanda had a lot to say about the harm that warfare was doing
to the environment. How much pollution was caused by a bomb
destroying a building? Why, in a world where every day new
drugs were being developed to prolong life, should so much
military force be deployed on a daily basis with a view to
curtailing it?

I apologized for having to keep the conversation short. And I
was sorry not to be there in person to see that she actually ate
something.

It never occurred to me to drive up to London. The traffic, parking
. . . I had taken the heavily loaded Yeti up a few times when we
were kitting out the Herne Hill flat, but would never choose it as
a transport option. I welcomed the hour and a half sitting on the
train. A rare opportunity just to read. At one stage I might have
said 'a rare opportunity to be out of contact for work problems',
but of course mobile phones put paid to that precious solitude.

It struck me as I travelled on the Tube from Victoria to Highbury
and Islington that Chloe Carter had quite a nerve. Being on
television clearly gave her a sense of entitlement. Our meeting
was completely on her terms. She had suggested it and never for
a moment seemed to have considered the hassle for me of getting
from Chichester to North London.

If our encounter had been for any other reason, I might have
got angry about how she'd set it up without any thought for my
convenience. But, since the meeting concerned what increasingly
I found myself thinking of as my investigation into Humph's
death, I didn't mind at all.

The studio was a short walk from the Tube station in a modern
office block which could have housed any kind of business. Back
in the day when Oliver had dealings about television animation
projects, meetings would take place in companies' central premises. BBC, ITV, Channel 4. Now, as much production as possible
was farmed out to independent studios.

I was buzzed into an unadorned reception area (no stills from the broadcasters' greatest hits). A languid girl behind a desk checked a clipboard and confirmed that I was expected. She summoned another, equally languid, girl who took me to the lift and escorted me to basement level where the studios were. A third girl, also languid, took me to the dressing room with 'Chloe Carter' on the door, and knocked.

'Come in.' The voice had lost its onscreen empathy. It was sharp and dictatorial.

I was ushered into the presence. Chloe Carter was having her make-up removed by one acolyte. Another stood with a tray of hairdresser's paraphernalia, ready to transform the black helmet into a more relaxed street look. Their mistress behaved as if they were invisible.

She behaved as if I was invisible too. She was on her mobile, deep in conversation about some other television project. She must have called out the 'Come in' in the middle of her chat. And now I had been admitted, I was going to have to wait till she finished the call. I deposited myself on a vacant chair.

'Yes, well do pressure them to make their minds up, Gwen,' she was saying. 'If they don't commission it quickly, we'll lose the topicality. OK, well, make that call. I'll be here for, I don't know, another twenty minutes. Yeah, see ya.'

Chloe Carter pressed the red button on her phone, then dismissed the make-up girl and hairdresser with a wave of her hand. 'I'll call you when you can come back.'

Now it was just the two of us in the dressing room, Chloe gave me no greeting or offer of a drink. She just said, 'We've really got to stop Mum talking about murder.'

'Who're you afraid of her talking to about it?'

'Anyone. So many people are on social media these days. Humph was a well-known person. Not any longer the media darling he wanted to be, but he still had a profile. Mum's got showbiz contacts. It's only a matter of time before she says something to one of them about her murder theory. Then it'll very quickly go viral.'

'Do you think it will? The suicide word hasn't been mentioned anywhere in the press, so why should the murder one?'

'OK, the whole affair's being very well managed by Humph's

agents – television and literary – and that'll give us a bit of breathing space until the inquest. When that verdict's announced, the news will be all over everywhere. And it's very important that that verdict is one of suicide.'

'Why is it so important?'

'Because it's the truth!' She fixed on me her 'I am a serious crusading journalist' look.

'How do you know that, Chloe?'

'Because Humph was always talking about suicide.'

'Not according to your mother.'

'She's only saying that because, for some reason, she's obsessed with her murder theory. He was always moaning about how dreadful his situation was, particularly in recent years when he wasn't getting any telly work. "If things go on like this, I'm going to top myself." God knows how many times I've heard him say that. And he always did love the grand gesture. No, there's no question about it. Humph killed himself.'

'Hm.' I digested that for a moment, then moved in a different direction. 'I get the impression your relationship with your father wasn't always easy.'

'That's an understatement, Ellen.' Oh good, she did at least remember my name. 'It always was quite abrasive. Humph didn't like being in the company of people who were brighter than he was. I often think that's why he married Mum.'

Ouch. Further proof, if any were needed, that Chloe Carter had a sharp tongue on her.

'Even when I was a kid, I didn't let him get away with stuff. At times he was full of shit, and I used to tell him so. He didn't like that. Couldn't stand criticism of any kind. So, things between us were always quite volatile. And then, when I started to make my way in television, he didn't like that one bit. Direct competition in his own backyard? No, no, no.'

'You know I've seen the birthday lunch video?'

'Yes, Mum told me.'

'I could see how he was undermining you there.'

'Oh, that was mild. It all got a lot worse as his career imploded and mine just went up and up. He claimed never to have watched my show. Sheer jealousy. His time in the sun was over, and I had all this.'

She preened herself as she gestured around what seemed to me a pretty basic concrete-walled dressing room. But, obviously, for Chloe Carter it symbolized a whole lot more.

'And every time my career made another advance, Humph showed less interest in it. I mean, this show is only a stepping stone. Already, I've been booked to make a series of documentaries on, you know, serious issues. And I've been in talks with some industry people about actually fronting a chat show.

'The prospect of that really destroyed Humph. From the moment I first mentioned the proposal, he just wouldn't listen. The thought of our skills and achievements being compared in the same arena . . . he couldn't cope with the idea. Probably just as well he won't be around to see that happen.'

I was taken aback by the callousness and arrogance of her words. 'Are you saying that his rivalry with you was a reason why he might have taken his own life?'

'No, that'd be an awful thing to say.' She gave a properly chastened look to the invisible camera. 'I'd feel terrible if I thought that was the case.' Though I could see the idea was not without appeal to her. 'But it's something that happens to a lot of people as they get older. There's less demand than there used to be for their skills. And, at the same time, there's a new younger generation coming up who do what the fogeys used to do rather better than they did. I mean, Humph used often to say – dramatically, of course – that he was in the elephants' graveyard. Waiting, as ever, for someone to contradict him. Which, of course, nobody did . . . because it was true.'

Time for me to change tack. 'Have you talked to your sister about his death?'

The idea seemed incongruous to her. 'No. Why should I have done?'

'I thought you might be interested to know her views on the subject.'

'You mean whether it was suicide or not?'

'Yes. She must have an opinion.'

'I wouldn't be so sure about that,' said Chloe bitchily. 'Not big on opinions, Little Miss Domesticity. Her normal reaction has always been to think what Humph told her to think.'

'Well, she can't do that now, can she?'

'No.' Chloe was thoughtful for a moment. 'She would think whatever reflected best on our father.'

'So, probably not suicide?'

'Probably not.' She spoke slowly, as though this was the first time she'd thought about her sister's reaction to their father's death. 'No, Kirsty wouldn't like the idea of suicide. Too messy for her. She doesn't like anything that discredits the myth of a united happy family.'

'Even when the alternative is murder?' I asked. 'Isn't that generally thought to be rather messy too?'

'Kirsty wouldn't think of murder. She'd close her mind to it. She closes her mind to anything that she thinks might upset her.'

Every word Chloe said strengthened the impression I'd already got of the sisters' relationship. 'And what about Garth?'

'What about Garth?'

'What might Garth's view be of his father-in-law's death?'

'Garth, the man who has donated to my sister the surname *Wickens*, has no views on anything. Kirsty deliberately married someone so wimpy that he'd never be a challenge to her in any area of her life. And now she's stuck with keeping him, paying all the family bills. Serve her right.'

'He's a writer, isn't he?'

That prompted a derisive laugh. 'He calls himself a writer. And he has all the necessary qualifications to be a writer, except for that vital detail of ever having written anything.'

'Ah.'

'He goes off every morning to a local café. With his laptop. The theory is that he's writing the great novel. He's been doing that for quite a while, though. I think all he does is chat about football with the other customers.'

'Right.' Increasingly, I was becoming convinced that I must get in touch with the sister and brother-in-law. There had to be more to them than Chloe implied. And their views could only help my investigation.

I changed tack again. 'Presumably, you knew about your father's drinking habits? The bottle of Famous Grouse in the desk drawer?'

'Yes, of course I did. The whole family knew. And he told anyone else who was prepared to listen. It was part of the image

he wanted to project. The hard-drinking journalist.' She looked
at me with new suspicion. 'Oh my God, you're not checking me
out as a potential murderer, are you?'

I shrugged. 'Just considering all the possibilities.'

'The only possibility,' Chloe Carter said with flat finality, 'is
that my father took his own life.'

'About the magazine article . . .' I pressed on. 'The one that
has been interpreted as a suicide note. Did you know about its
existence before—?'

I was interrupted by the dressing room door being thrown
open to admit a woman in her thirties, whose clothes and body
language oozed confidence.

'Hi, Chloe,' she said. 'I've just talked to Baz about the proposal.
He's got the commissioner's ear. He says it's just the kind of
content they're looking for, deadly serious but, you know, human.
They'll greenlight it the minute the verdict's announced. It could
be a big break for you, particularly given the—'

'Gwen.' Chloe interrupted with some force. 'Gwen, this is
Ellen.'

The newcomer became aware of me for the first time. Oh, hi.'
She reached across to shake my hand. 'Gwen Martino,' she said.

'Ellen Curtis.'

'We're nearly done here, Gwen.' Chloe turned on me a look
which was my exit cue. 'Be in touch, eh? If we need to talk
further about things . . . well, you've got my mobile.'

'Sure.'

And, rather unceremoniously, I was dismissed from the presence of Chloe Carter.

It was awful not to be looking forward to meeting the son I
hadn't seen for four months. But I'm afraid that was the case. I
desperately wanted to see Ben. But I wanted to see him on his
own, when he could talk to me directly, tell me what was really
going on in his complicated mind.

Seeing him in the company of the exotic Layla Valdez – and
my mother Fleur – was not my idea of a dream scenario.

As it turned out there were five of us at lunch, but the additional
participant did not make things any easier for me. This was

Layla's publicist, a sharp-suited Californian called Sydnee. Her
role was half minder, half censor. She intervened far too often
when she thought her charge might be, either, offended, or, about
to reveal something about *Virgins of the Fall* which was still
embargoed.

The venue was an exclusive private club in Soho. Not one of
the obvious ones I had heard of, like the Groucho or Soho House.
It was too exclusive and private for anyone except its members
to know the name. The entrance looked like the main door of
someone's private house (assuming that someone was rich enough
to live where the property prices in London were at their highest).

I had told Fleur that I had a London appointment earlier in
the day, though I hadn't specified who it was with. In fact, I
hadn't mentioned anything to her about the Carter family.
Fortunately, because my connection with them was to do with
SpaceWoman, my mother would not have expressed any interest,
anyway. Just made another reference to my 'cleaning'.

Had she known that my work had introduced me to the recently
deceased Humphrey Carter, she would probably have reacted
differently. He had, after all, for a while been showbiz royalty.
I had heard Fleur say more than once – and untruthfully – that
the producers had wanted her to guest on *Humphrey Carter
Interviews* . . . but, 'the dates they offered never worked for me.'

So, I was quite glad she didn't know my connection. Fleur
Bonnier considered that her career history gave her the right to
monopolize anyone she met who was 'in the business'.

Which was exactly what I feared she would proceed to do
with Layla Valdez.

How right I was. Fleur, who, I later discovered, had booked a car
all the way from Chichester on Kenneth's business account, had
arrived at the club before me. They had gone straight to the table
and, by the time I got there, my mother was putting everyone at
their ease (at least I'm sure that's what she thought she was doing).

Layla Valdez was, it has to be said, stunning. I hadn't been
too proud to do a little online research on her. I'd even watched
the odd episode of television series she'd been in. And, though
in both the stills and the film footage she'd looked wonderful, I
knew how much work by stylists, hairdressers and make-up artists

would have gone into creating those images. I was prepared for the reality to be a little underwhelming.

But I was wrong (though I hope not so mean-spirited as to be disappointed). Layla was a natural beauty. Perfect complexion, naturally black hair (maybe some Latin inheritance that came with the name 'Valdez').

Her voice was charming too. Though she had taken on American accents for the shows I had seen her in, in the company of fellow Brits she reverted to her native Liverpudlian. And when she spoke to Sydnee, it was in a strange mix of the two.

As I was ushered to the table, Layla sprang up to meet me. She gave me a firm hug, which brought me into her aura of expensive perfume, and said, 'Ellen, it's so good to meet you at last. Benjamin's told me so much about you!'

I wondered if that was true. When Ben's on a high – and, so far as I knew, he'd been on a high ever since he'd got together with Layla – he disassociates himself from his lows. So, it was likely that he'd said very little about his mother, who'd witnessed so many of his breakdowns. I was quite possibly tainted with the brush of his depression, a part of his past that he had grown out of.

Layla's hug was followed by Ben's, which felt somehow distant and artificial. What he was wearing reinforced that impression. Clothes have never featured high on my son's list of priorities. He had always been happy to slouch around in sweatshirts with jeans or jogging bottoms. So, to see him in a coral linen suit, worn over a navy blue T-shirt, was something of a culture shock.

And the shock was not decreased by his saying a fulsome, 'Good to see ya, Mom!'

Ben occasionally calls me 'Mum'. More often, he opts for something which started off as an ironic joke between us but became part of our relationship – 'Ma'. He has never before called me 'Mom'.

'I think we'd better order,' said a peremptory Sydnee. 'Layla's got back-to-back interviews all afternoon.'

A waiter was summoned before I'd even had a chance to look at the menu.

'Just main courses,' Sydnee dictated. 'Because of the time pressure.'

She was distracted by a ping from her large ultramodern phone. It was the first of many such distractions that happened during the short lunch. Sydnee made no apologies for her constant use of the phone. The calls were more important than the company she was in.

It was very definitely her show. To my surprise, she ordered for her client. 'Layla,' she told the waiter, 'will be having the spice-crusted tofu with kumquat radish salad. And Ben . . .' She looked at him and sighed. 'Be the usual beetroot and quinoa burger, will it, Benjamin?'

'You betcha,' my son replied.

I know a mother should be pleased to see her son eating healthily, but I couldn't help remembering, rather wistfully, how Ben used to relish the massive fry-ups I would cook for him.

Sydnee turned to my mother. 'And, Fleur, what would you like? As you see, they have non-vegan options.'

'Oh, well, actually,' came the astonishing reply, 'I do find I'm eating decreasing amounts of meat these days.' That was a downright lie. My mother surveyed the vegan options, using all her acting skills to make it look as if they were familiar, before pronouncing, 'I'll have the shakshuka with tofu "eggs".' Grudgingly, I had to give her full marks for sounding like she'd ever spoken those words before.

Sydnee's interrogator's beam focused on me. I wasn't being deliberately perverse. It was just what I felt like. I asked for the sirloin steak. Rare.

'And I'll have the cloud ear mushroom salad,' said Sydnee, in a tone of dismissal to the waiter.

'Any drinks?' he asked.

'Just sparkling mineral water,' said Sydnee.

I looked at Fleur. She could pretend to be a convincing vegan, but could she pretend to be a woman who didn't like a glass of wine with her lunch? She looked at me with something like pleading.

'I think we might have some wine,' I said, flipping the menu to look at the list. 'Fleur will have a large glass of the New Zealand Chardonnay . . . and I'll have a large glass of the Chilean Merlot.'

The waiter departed. Sydnee was preoccupied by a text.

Needless to say, it was Fleur who launched the next stage of the conversation. 'Oh, you must be so excited, Layla, to be going to see the finished product of the movie you've been working on so long.'

'Well, it is kind of exciting, yes. Mind you, I have seen it before.'

'Yes, but for the first time with an audience.'

'I guess.'

'Oh,' said Fleur, and it was a long 'Oh.' 'I remember the butterflies I used to get before the premières of my movies.'

I couldn't recall any of hers actually having premières. I'd got the impression that, while some motion pictures are launched, those British films of the 1980s which featured Fleur Bonnier more, sort of, slipped off their moorings while nobody was watching. They certainly never made it to the Odeon, Leicester Square.

'And I knew it was silly,' my mother continued, 'because at that stage there's absolutely nothing you can do about it. The whole thing's been in the can for ages, all shot and edited. But I still always used to get a tingle. And that was—'

Sydnee cut across her to report her latest information. 'The producers want you on the red carpet on your own, Layla. Just with the other stars.'

'OK.' Layla looked across at Ben, whose face wore a look of disappointment I remembered from primary school days. She reached to take his hand. 'Don't worry, honey. They want to focus on the movie.'

'Yes, but I'd like to be there with you.'

'Benjamin, it's not a big deal.'

'I bet Craig and Zeezee will be there on the carpet together.'

'Of course they will. They're both in the movie. Anyway, they were a couple before we started shooting.'

This news didn't make Ben look any less disgruntled. I couldn't believe it. Here was my son, whom I had seen on many occasions so lacking in confidence that he literally couldn't get out of bed, and he was throwing a hissy fit about not being allowed on the red carpet for a film première.

I tried to rationalize my reaction. I should be happy for him. How many times had I prayed to the God I don't believe in that he would gain some self-belief, that he would lose the fatal negativity which bedevilled his and his father's lives? Now that my wish appeared to have been granted, why was I feeling so churlish about it?

I was also upset that, since the first fulsome greeting, Ben hadn't addressed another word directly to me. He'd responded to Layla and Fleur and kind of included me in general conversation, but he hadn't talked to me. My son hadn't talked to me.

Sydnee took another call. She listened briefly, then said, 'Nine o'clock tomorrow morning at the hotel.' Switched off the phone and turned to Layla. 'That's your therapist rescheduled.'

'Great,' said the actress.

'Oh, I do so believe in therapy,' said Fleur. 'Of course, I've had mental health issues.' Both sentences were blatant lies. The only thing wrong with my mother's mind was that she sometimes thought she was rather more important, in the scheme of things, than she actually was. She was also extremely unsympathetic to genuine mental illness, having more than once expressed the opinion that Oliver and Ben should 'snap out of it'.

'It's the American way,' said Layla. 'Not like here. Here, you have a problem, you live with it. In the States, you have a problem, you go to someone who can sort it out for you.'

I wondered if that's what she'd been recommending to Ben. Was his new apparent equilibrium the result of some genius therapist? God knows, I'd taken him to enough mental health professionals over the years, but none of their ministrations had resulted in more than temporary improvement in his mental health. The depression had always returned. But, if the new stateside regime had worked, I wasn't about to knock it.

The food arrived. Seeing what the others were presented with, I was very glad I'd gone for the steak option. It was beautifully cooked, with huge triple-cooked chips, mushrooms, onions and leaf spinach. The Merlot was excellent, too. As I had the first sip, I decided that I would definitely have a second glass. It was so rare that I had a day when I wasn't going to have to drive at some point, I would take full advantage of it.

I was amused to see the doubtful eye that Fleur cast on her the shakshuka with tofu 'eggs'. Not to mention the envious one she cast at my steak.

The lunch was by no means silent. There was a lot of conversation, but I didn't feel part of any of it. Layla and Ben – or Benjamin, as she insisted on calling him – seemed very together, talking and giggling about people I didn't know (though I believe most of them were, in some context, famous). When she wasn't taking calls, Sydnee kept giving instructions to Layla about what she should and shouldn't say to the press that afternoon. And Fleur elbowed her way in whenever she saw an opportunity (she was very good at seeing such opportunities). I said little.

When the waiter passed, I gratefully ordered my second glass of wine. Fleur took the opportunity to ask for another Chardonnay.

She had just been questioning the publicist about what her job entailed. Sydnee seemed disinclined to get involved in irrelevant conversation, but Layla answered in cosy Liverpudlian, 'She's my lifeline, Fleur. Always looks after me, and keeps the press off my back. Monitors my social media, too. How was it you described yourself when we first worked together, Sydnee?'

'Ego mechanic,' came the short reply.

'Basically,' Layla went on, 'I'm allowed to get on with the business of being an actor and Sydnee handles all the other stuff.'

'Oh, how wonderful!' said Fleur. 'That's exactly what I need, as an actor. What I've always needed.'

'Are you still acting?' asked Layla.

'Oh, God, yes. Though I have been doing less in recent years.'

That was something of an overstatement. Less? She hadn't done any paid work for at least a decade.

'The trouble is,' Fleur continued, 'in our business . . .' How she loved identifying with Layla Valdez '. . . there's a perception that one's range diminishes as one matures. Whereas, of course, the very opposite is true. One develops as an artiste. One's skills improve, one is more ready than ever to tackle any kind of role.

'But do casting directors see it like that? Do they hell? As a breed, they're very short-sighted. I mean, I'm ready to work at the drop of a hat . . . if only I was offered the right parts. All the scripts I get sent feature such dreadfully stereotyped characters.'

It wasn't my place to ask when she had last been offered a script. Of any kind. I knew the answer, though.

'Well, Fleur,' said Ben, 'what you really need is a publicist like Sydnee to get your career back on track.'

'Oh yes, Ben darling, that would be perfect! But would she do it for me?'

'You could ask her,' said Layla.

Fleur turned her most winsome, beseeching face on the publicist. But before she could utter a word, Sydnee consulted her watch and said, 'We need to cut this short. Layla, you've got to be in make-up in five.'

I firmly believe – thank God – that Fleur didn't see the looks exchanged between Ben and Layla as he suggested Sydnee might work as a publicist for her. I did, though. They were sending her up. They were making fun of her.

And, in spite of all the annoyances she had caused me over the years, that upset me a lot. I found myself feeling protective of the old boot.

TWELVE

It seemed only a matter of seconds and they were gone. I had offered to contribute to the bill, but Sydnee snapped, 'It's covered.'

Layla Valdez gave me and Fleur big hugs, saying it had been 'wonderful' to meet us.

Ben gave us equally enthusiastic hugs which felt meaningless. 'Fab to see you, Mom,' he said, on a giggle.

And that was it. The son I hadn't seen for four months. I hadn't had a single significant word with him. And the last thing I'd seen was him making fun of my mother.

'If it's covered,' said Fleur slyly, 'there's nothing to stop us ordering another glass of wine.'

Normally, I would have turned down the suggestion. But I felt so shaken and hurt that I agreed.

'Well, our Ben's landed on his feet there, hasn't he?' said Fleur.

'She seemed very nice,' I said, unable to stop the words from sounding mean-spirited.

'You see, Ellen darling, that's all he's needed. The right girl-friend – and suddenly all those mental health issues you worry about so much have just gone. Vanished.'

'I hope you're right.'

'Of course I'm right. Layla is famous and the fact that she wants to be with Ben has solved all his confidence problems. I recognize what's happening. Some of my boyfriends, way back, got an enormous charge of being seen out with me, with a famous actor.'

Just when I'm on the edge of feeling sympathetic towards Fleur, she says something like that and my attitude changes completely. 'But none of those relationships survived, did they?' I said with some edge.

'They were finite,' she said with affected melancholy. 'By their very nature. Young love is a fragile flower. I was at the stage of my life when I was eager for experience, for excitement, for adventure.' I wondered whether she was quoting from some play she'd been in. She often did. 'I wasn't mature enough to be faithful, back then.'

The question that formed in my mind was: Were you ever? But, shrewdly, in my mind was where I left it.

The waiter brought our refills.

'When we've had these,' said Fleur, 'I'll summon the car. We can have a nice chat on the way back to Chichester.'

'Oh, I hadn't told you,' I responded. 'I'm not going straight back. There's something else I have to do in London.'

Fleur's expression was tight with curiosity. But I didn't tell her what I was going to do.

I hadn't informed Jools even that I was going to be in London overnight, but she'd expressed the likelihood that she'd be staying in Worthing, so I reckoned she wouldn't even be aware of my absence. I hadn't asked any questions about who the attraction was in Worthing, but it seemed that she had been seeing a real person, rather than someone online. Promising news. It wasn't a development in her social life that I worried about.

What had happened to cause her breakdown in the Herne Hill flat, on the other hand, was something I did worry about. A lot.

And, for the time being, I tried to make that preoccupation shut my mind to worries about whether I still had any kind of relationship with my son.

I was rarely in London so, after I left the club, I thought I'd have a look at some of the shops round Oxford Circus. I wandered rather pathetically from store to store, my mind too full to focus on what was on offer. I maybe did that for an hour or two, feeling uncharacteristically listless.

Then I noticed it was getting dark. I went to catch the Tube, without having bought anything.

I had keys. Though it had always been very much Jools's place, she'd agreed, somewhat grudgingly, that I needed access. I had, after all, lent her the money for the deposit.

I'd taken the Tube to Blackfriars, then the train to the graffiti-covered Herne Hill station. A short walk took me to an Edwardian house on three storeys, each of which had been converted into a flat. As I got close, I couldn't help remembering the last time I'd been there.

Some months before, on a Sunday evening, worried by total lack of communication from Jools and her refusal to answer her phone, I had driven up from Chichester. I found her on the sofa, where she'd been for three days, not eating anything but occasionally sipping water. She had a bloody dressing over injuries to her face.

As I drove her home that evening, for the first time since his suicide, she did actually talk about Oliver. She also talked about her own life and how it had unravelled. The image she'd projected to me – and particularly to Fleur – was of a successful career girl in the world of fashion. She wrote for various online publications and was kept busy in a whirl of product launches and catwalk shows. She was building up a profile as an influencer.

I still hadn't really worked out how much of this was true and how much fabrication. Although we talked much more now she was living and working with me in Chichester, the precise circumstances of her breakdown remained a no-go area. I didn't want to raise the subject for fear of triggering some kind of relapse. I guess I thought Jools would tell me about it when she was good and ready. Though she showed no signs of being good and ready. Maybe she thought putting the past behind her was a necessary step in her recovery.

All I really knew was that she had been the victim of online trolling. How near she had ever been to gaining the status of an *influencer*, I had no idea. I do know that criticism of her looks on Twitter had led to her succumbing to a botched nose job by an unregulated surgeon in Budapest. Hence the bloodied dressing.

It was on her return from Hungary that she had taken to the sofa. What would have happened if I hadn't found her three days later, I tremble to think of. All I knew was that, whereas I'd considered Ben to be the vulnerable one, and his sister permanently protected by a carapace she'd built up against the toughness of the world outside, I now had two children with mental health issues. Given the circumstances of their father's death, that was

hardly surprising. Jools's suffering had just taken longer to mani-
fest itself.

As I used my key to enter the Herne Hill flat, its emptiness
was almost tangible. I got the strong impression that no one else
had been in there since Jools and I left. There was certainly a
fine layer on every surface of that London dust which somehow
circumvents the most assiduously fitted double glazing.

I wandered round the place, searching hopefully for clues to
my daughter's life.

I didn't find much. Apart from the dust, the flat was in immacu-
late order. There had always been an innate tidiness about Jools,
in marked contrast to the permanent state of chaos that surrounded
her brother. Her almost pathological neatness was one of the
reasons why she had slotted so readily into the work of
SpaceWoman.

There was one room in the flat, however, which still confused
me. When I'd stayed with her on an occasion before her breakdown, Jools had given up her bed for me and slept on the sofa,
although there was a second bedroom. The following morning,
after she'd gone out, I'd furtively explored the spare room.

Then, there had been no bed or other furniture, just rows of
garment racks. It was exactly the same on my latest visit, though
this time, as in the other rooms, there was a film of London dust
over everything. All of the racks were full, hung with brand-new
clothes of the kind that were bought cheaply, worn a few times
and then, in many cases, ended up in landfill.

They represented an aspect of the fashion industry, of which
I, with my increasingly puritanical green values, disapproved
strongly.

Their presence raised the major question of where my daughter
had got them from. In conversations, particularly with Fleur,
Jools had gone on about the constant invitations she received to
fashion shows and the number of 'freebies', as an influential
journalist, she was given.

That, I had reckoned, explained the extensive wardrobe in the
spare room. But Jools's breakdown then cast doubt on that
assumption, along with many others. How much of the life she
described to Fleur and me was real, how much imagined? Or
had it started off real and then drifted into fantasy? How much

of her social contact had been with genuine friends, how much online?

This led directly to the next question. If none of the dresses in the spare room were actually freebies, had Jools bought them? And, if she had, where had she got the money from?

The same source which was paying her mortgage? The mysterious P. Driscoll?

In the flat above. Where he might be at that precise moment. I felt suddenly very nervous.

Because, to confront P. Driscoll was the reason why I had come to Herne Hill. While I was steeling myself for this encounter, my mobile pinged with a text. I was glad of the distraction, particularly when I saw that it came from Kirsty Wickens.

'Could you call me tomorrow morning between ten and twelve? There are things I need to talk to you about.'

That was good news. I had been thinking I'd have to contact Theresa to get a number for her younger daughter. But I'd been saved the trouble.

The trouble with P. Driscoll, though, remained to be resolved.

I had noticed before, when visiting Jools's flat, that there was a three-station entry system beside the front door. The name in the top slot was *Kumari*, the name in the bottom one, predictably enough, *Curtis*. And between them was *Driscoll*.

I had considered starting by pressing the outside buzzer. But then it struck me that, since I had access to the interior, someone was less likely to ignore a summons from a visitor on their immediate doorstep.

The staircase and the two landings survived from the previously undivided family house. I left Jools's flat, took a few deep breaths and then went up one flight of stairs. The door that faced me was identical to the one below, except for the number '2' rather than '1' on its letterbox. The bellpush to the side of the door was also in exactly the same position.

I pressed it. Nothing happened. I allowed a minute and pressed again.

I am quite experienced at this. In my SpaceWoman work, I'm often dealing with people who don't want to let me inside their homes. Their first reaction to a knock or a ring at the door is to do nothing.

I gave it five minutes and tried again. Silence. Whether or not there was anyone behind the impassive door I had no means of knowing.

And, for a moment, I questioned my approach. Maybe ringing at the inside door was a bad move. The occupant of the flat might wonder how their unannounced caller had got into the building.

I rang once again and achieved the same absence of response.

Still, there was something else I could try. I went up to the top floor and rang the bell of Flat 3. The door was opened only as far as a chain would allow, to reveal the wary face of an Indian man carrying a sleeping toddler.

'Mr Kumari?' I asked.

'Yes?' He was instinctively suspicious of someone he didn't recognize who'd managed to get past the front door.

'My name's Ellen Curtis,' I said quickly before he could shut me out. 'Mother of Jools, who owns the ground floor flat.'

That relaxed him. He knew my daughter. But he still didn't undo the door chain. He'd lived in London long enough to be wary of strangers.

'Is she OK?' he asked. 'I don't seem to have seen her for a few weeks.'

'She's fine. Been away,' I said, not wishing to get into detailed explanations.

'Oh, good. Well, give her my best wishes.'

'Of course.' Funny, Jools had never said anything to me about the other residents in her building. But, come to that, I'd never asked her about them.

'I'm actually here,' I went on, 'because Jools wanted to get a message to Mr Driscoll in Flat 2.'

'Ah. Well, you'll be lucky.'

I was instantly alert. 'Why, has something happened to him?'

Through the narrow aperture, Mr Kumari shrugged. 'Nothing new has happened to him. Since we've lived here, he's always been difficult to make contact with.'

'In what way?'

'He doesn't answer the door when people ring the bell.'

'I've just experienced that. I assumed he was out.'

'Unlikely,' said Mr Kumari. 'He rarely goes out after dark.'

'What about during the daytime? Is he here then?'

'No. He goes out every morning at eight. He comes back at six. And the only reason he comes out of the flat in the evening is if he's got an Amazon delivery.'

'Oh?'

'And he gets quite a few of them. Often during the day there'll be a pile of small boxes on the doormat.'

'Do you know where he goes during the day?' Mr Kumari shrugged. 'Has he got a job?'

'I don't know. I don't know anything about the man. I have tried speaking to him but he never replies. At first I thought it might be a racist reaction, but now I think he is the same with everyone. He doesn't talk to people.'

'Look, would you mind if I gave you my mobile number? If you see Mr Driscoll, could you give it to him and ask him to call me?'

Mr Kumari shrugged. 'Give it, by all means. But, as I say, he's very unlikely to respond.'

'Please.'

'OK.'

'And would you mind giving me your number too?'

'Jools has got it. We exchanged numbers when she moved in.'

'Yes, but she had her phone stolen,' I lied inventively. 'I'd be grateful if you could . . .'

He nodded. No skin off his nose. He gave me the two numbers.

I began, 'And I wonder if—'

At that moment, the child in his arms stretched and started to cry. 'I am sorry. I must change her nappy.'

'Well, thank you very much for your—'

The door had closed before I could finish the sentence.

So, I would be staying in Herne Hill overnight. I tried Mr P. Driscoll's number and was unsurprised when he didn't answer. I didn't leave a message. I decided I'd try to speak to him when he left the house at eight in the morning. Though, if he didn't talk to anyone, why would he make an exception for me?

More interesting – and more disturbing – was how my daughter had contacted him, why he had taken to paying her bills, and what was the nature of the relationship between them.

With that to worry about – and with the feeling that I no longer had any connection with my son, I did not anticipate a restful night.

THIRTEEN

was right. I didn't sleep well. After a restless evening watching irrelevant television, I'd retired to Jools's bed, which still had the sheets on from when she'd last slept there. There was even dried blood on the pillow from the leaking dressing put on her nose in Budapest.

I do have standards. Normally, I would have changed the bedding straight away, but I felt too drained and lethargic to do even that. The same inertia stopped me from going out to one of the local restaurants or getting something to eat from the supermarket. Apart from anything else, I was still full of my expensive lunchtime steak.

The result was that the next morning I woke up (which must mean that I'd slept a bit) absolutely ravenous. There was nothing in the fridge (which I hadn't thought to switch off when I'd last been in the flat) except for some elderly cheese and a wizened lemon.

I sat at the kitchen table, bag and keys at the ready, waiting for the sound of a door opening upstairs. And I tried to rationalize what my approach to the mysterious Mr Driscoll should be.

As Mr Kumari had implied, he was a creature of strict habit. On the dot of eight o'clock, I heard the double click of a door opening and closing above me. I had by then decided not to confront him on the stairs. The information I had received from his upstairs neighbour was suggesting a character profile for Mr P. Driscoll to me. And it was one with which I was very familiar. My SpaceWoman work put me in touch with a lot of recluses.

So, I knew that, if I intercepted my quarry inside the building, he was quite likely to scuttle back into his flat and stay there till long after I had had to give up surveillance. In the open – unless he had a car arranged to pick him up on his doorstep – I had a much better chance of getting to talk to him.

I waited until I heard his footsteps reach the hallway, then opened Jools's door a fraction, so that I would recognize who I should be following. As soon as the front door clicked shut, I was out of the flat and off in pursuit.

Mr Driscoll's back view was so unremarkable that it almost looked as though he'd deliberately set out to look unremarkable. He was of middling height, dressed in dark blue jeans too long for his legs so that they'd been scuffed by the heels of his black trainers. He wore a quilted jacket, also dark blue, with a hood, though he hadn't got it up. The bald circle on top of his head was surrounded by wisps of ginger-turning-to-white hair. He carried something fairly heavy in a beige canvas tote bag.

Not only unremarkable, but also unprepossessing. A chill ran through me. What hold had this man got over my daughter? The horrible phrase 'sex for rent' bubbled uneasily back up to the surface of my mind.

I was confused. My mind should have been clearer about what I was going to do. I had found my quarry. He was in my sights. But my will seemed paralysed. What should my next action be? He wasn't walking in the direction of the station. Maybe he was going to a bus stop?

My indecision was ended by P. Driscoll's own movements. He went into a place called 'Kalkan Kaffee'. Its ethnicity was Turkish. Signs on the steamed-up windows offered a tantalizing selection of specials.

I was far enough behind for him not to feel as if he had been followed in. Incidentally, from the moment he left his flat, P. Driscoll had not once turned round to look behind him. He had no suspicions of me. I was just another anonymous person in the vast anonymity of London.

There was a small breakfast-time queue at the counter, mostly ordering takeaways, but he didn't join it. He went and sat at a corner table near a radiator. He did not remove his quilted jacket but took a laptop out of his tote bag and placed it on the table whose surface showed plasticized scenes of Istanbul. He switched on and was instantly absorbed by whatever appeared on the screen. His movements seemed almost ritualized. He had done this many times before.

My turn in the queue came. The smells emanating from the

kitchen made my hunger even sharper. I ordered a black Americano and saw from the menu that they did one of my favourite Turkish dishes. *Menemen*. Scrambled eggs, onions, peppers, chillies, garlic and a lot of other good stuff. I ordered it. Mothers stalking men who may have abused their daughters are allowed to eat. Need to eat, in fact.

From the way he called out orders to the kitchen, the man who served me appeared to be the owner of Kalkan Kaffee. He seemed surprised when I said I wanted to eat in. Apart from P. Driscoll's, few of the tables were occupied. That time of day, most of the customers were grabbing something to eat in the office.

I took a seat a couple of tables away from him. Then, as everyone does when they're left alone, I took out my mobile. Just to look busy. I'd checked my emails in the flat only minutes before. There were a couple of SpaceWoman enquiries which I'd emailed Jools to follow up on.

And there was the previous day's message from Kirsty Wickens. Very specific. Call between ten and twelve. Mustn't forget to do that. Mind you, it was still only eight-twenty.

My coffee arrived, delivered by a bright-eyed girl with black hair in a long ponytail. The owner's daughter? Very good coffee it was.

At the same time, she brought a coffee for P. Driscoll. Put it on the table to the side of his laptop. He acknowledged neither its arrival nor the waitress who'd brought it. So . . . he had a regular order. Getting what he wanted in Kalkan Kaffee now involved no personal interaction. But it must have done at some point. The first time he came in there . . .?

I had stationed myself at a table where I could see what P. Driscoll was doing without appearing to be watching him. But I still didn't know how I was actually going to make contact.

The girl came from the kitchen in our direction, carrying two plates. Mine was the *Menemen* which she put on my table with a bright grin. I thanked her and said it smelled wonderful. Which it did. The grin broadened.

His order was a breakfast. Full English, avoiding all of the Turkish dishes which featured such delights as smoked salmon and peppers. With his bacon, eggs, sausage, beans and fried bread, Mr Driscoll seemed to be a man of rigid habits.

The girl had her back to me when she put the plate down beside his laptop, so I couldn't see whether she smiled at him too. From his unchanging expression and his eyes' concentration on the laptop screen, I shouldn't think she bothered. Certainly, no words were exchanged.

Time for me to act. Now he'd actually got his breakfast in front of him, P. Driscoll wasn't about to move, was he?

I rose from my table and went towards his. 'Mr Driscoll . . .' I began. 'I am Jools Curtis's mother and I want to talk to you about—'

I'd been wrong. The arrival of his breakfast did not stop his departure. Folding his laptop and returning it to the tote bag in one movement, he immediately left Kalkan Kaffee.

The effect of my intervention had not pleased the proprietor. Leaving the queue waiting at the counter, he strode across to me and demanded in a thick accent, 'What did you say to him?'

'He didn't give me a chance to say anything.'

'He comes in here so that he won't be disturbed.'

'I didn't know that, did I?'

'But why did you talk to him?'

'He knows my daughter. He lives in the flat above hers.'

'Ah.' He seemed a little mollified. Maybe he approved of the family as an institution. 'Harika!' he called across to the pony-tailed girl. Following his instructions in Turkish, she instantly took over serving the waiting customers.

'He is one of my best customers,' the proprietor grumbled. 'If he doesn't come back, I lose a lot of money.'

I don't know why I felt combative, but I said, 'Surely losing one Full English breakfast order, even if it happens every day, is not going to put you out of business?'

'You do not understand,' he said. His mood shifted and, with a shy smile, he said, 'I am Mehmet.'

'Ellen.'

'I have special arrangement with the gentleman who has just left.'

'Do you know his name?' He shook his head.

'It's Mr P. Driscoll. I don't know what the "P" stands for.'

'Ah.' The fact that I knew the name seemed to ease Mehmet's suspicions of me. 'You are the first person I have met who knows him.' I didn't stop him to mention my rather tenuous claim to 'knowing'. 'He is always here on his own.'

'So, he comes here for breakfast the same time every morning?' My character profile of P. Driscoll was beginning to fill out a little.

'Yes,' Mehmet replied, 'but not just breakfast. He stays here for lunch and has an evening meal before we close at six.'

'Every day?'

'Every day.'

'Including the weekends?'

'Including the weekends. Kalkan Kaffee is open the same hours every day of the week.'

'And what does Mr Driscoll do in here all day?'

Mehmet shrugged. 'He has his laptop open, with the lead plugged in over there. What he is doing on it I don't know.'

'And he just sits here all day?

'All day.'

'Don't you find his behaviour rather odd?'

Another shrug. 'I do not judge him. There is room for every kind of person in the world.'

His words so accurately reflected my own views that he almost made me feel guilty for the suspicions I'd been harbouring about the mysterious Mr Driscoll. Then I reminded myself what he might have been doing with my daughter.

'Do you have any means of contacting him?' I asked.

A glint of suspicion returned to Mehmet's eye as he said, 'If he owns the flat above your daughter, then you know where he lives.'

'Yes. But I've tried contacting him there without success.'

A wry grin from Mehmet. 'Then I think, from that and what happened here this morning, he doesn't want to see you.'

'Maybe not. But I do need to see him.'

It must have been the note of desperation in my voice that swayed Mehmet. 'I have an email address for him. Some months back we had a flood in the kitchen and had to close for three days. The gentleman was very put out and insisted on giving me his email address, so that I could warn him if anything similar ever happened again.'

'Would you mind passing it on to me?' I pleaded.

He nodded. 'I'll get it. It's on the laptop in the kitchen.' He looked across at the lengthening queue of breakfast-seekers. 'I must go and help my daughter.'

'Of course.'

He picked up the unclaimed Full English and looked down at my metal dish of *Menemen*, whose contents were beginning to congeal. 'And I will get you another of these.'

'Really, don't bother.'

'I will bother,' he said proudly. 'Turkish food must be served properly. *Menemen* should be piping hot.'

'Well, thank you.' As he turned towards the counter, I asked, 'Do you think P. Driscoll will come back?'

'I think so. I feel he is a man slow to change his habits.'

Spot on, I thought. Mehmet's analysis of the man's character coincided with my own.

'I hope so, anyway,' he said with feeling.

'Oh?'

'The reason I wish him to return is that he is unusual among my customers. Most of them stay here with their laptops, making one cup of coffee last for hours. The gentleman who has just left pays me very well for the privilege of spending his days in my café.'

'More than just for the food he orders?'

'Very much more,' said Mehmet as he went to join his daughter at the counter.

A few minutes later my *Menemen* was delivered by Mehmet's daughter. They hadn't just heated up the one that had gone cold. This was a fresh helping, sizzling in its metal dish on top of an oval wooden board. she also put down a page from a food order pad, on which an email address had been written.

'Thank you, Harika,' I said and was rewarded by another of her beautiful smiles.

The *Menemen* was divine. The best I've ever tasted.

And, as my tastebuds cooed with delight, I thought about the mysterious Mr Driscoll.

Such recluses, my work at SpaceWoman had taught me, could be extremely dangerous.

I went back to the flat. I hadn't left any of my belongings, but I still felt I should check whether P. Driscoll had returned there.

Though, I reckoned ruefully, it would be virtually impossible to
know that for sure. Our encounter at Kalkan Kaffee made it even
less likely that he would respond to a ring at his doorbell. So, I
wouldn't have a clue whether he actually was in residence or
not.

As it turned out, I was lucky. I did get a pointer. Entering the
building's main door, I saw on the mat an Amazon parcel small
enough to get through the letterbox. Which definitely hadn't been
there when I left the building. It was addressed to Perry Driscoll.

That gave me two bits of information. His first name, which
was useful. And also, given how quickly Mr Kumari told me the
recluse usually picked up his Amazon deliveries, the fact that he
hadn't come back to his flat.

I went up to Jools's, where I was drawn ineluctably to the
spare room, that warehouse of cheap dresses. What did it mean?
What had been my daughter's motivation for building up the
collection? In some way I felt sure it had something to do with
her breakdown. And where did the evasive P. Driscoll fit into the
scenario?

There were no two ways about it. I would have to ask her
directly. Yet, even as I had the thought, I knew precisely how
difficult that would be. Why is it that, the closer you are to a
person, the harder it becomes to ask them straightforward
questions?

I felt restless. Maybe a coffee would help . . .? Jools had a
good modern machine, but exhaustive searches of her kitchen
cupboards revealed no pods to go in it.

I went into the sitting room and switched on the television. I
couldn't remember when I'd last watched any daytime stuff.
Determined never to have a set in my bedroom, it wasn't a part
of my morning schedule. That consisted of coffee, shower, putting
on my SpaceWoman livery, dab of make-up, wolfing down a
hasty but substantial breakfast (who knew when I would eat
next?) and off in the Yeti to face the challenges of the day ahead.

Ergh . . . The breakfast television presenters, one of each
gender, were relentlessly jolly. I had, needless to say, never heard
of either of them. But I suppose they must have commanded
some level of celebrity. Doing the same job as Chloe Carter.
There must be people out there who enjoy it. I would have

switched off, had I not heard the relentlessly jolly female presenter say, '. . . and we know her best as the feisty Micky Trenchard from *Wanderers*, but she's now moved to the big time in the States. And last night saw the premiere of her first feature film, *Virgins of the Fall*. So, welcome to our sofa . . . Layla Valdez!'

The camera found her, looking impossibly gorgeous for that time in the morning. 'It's a pleasure to be here,' she said, in her thickest Liverpudlian. Back on home soil, she wanted to show how little she'd been spoiled by success, how close she remained to her humble roots.

I couldn't stand it. Everything that I'd been shutting off since the previous day's lunch suddenly flooded into my mind. I switched off the television.

And, sitting on the sofa of my daughter's flat in Herne Hill, I cried.

I very rarely cry. Even in the bruising aftermath of Oliver's suicide, though I had been through every kind of hell, there was very little crying involved. And any that was done was done in private. There's some mechanism in my body which prevents me from crying in front of people.

But that morning, reminded how completely I had lost my son, I sat on my daughter's sofa and cried.

I allowed half an hour, then tidied myself up. Tissues, splashes of cold water over my face and a little more defensive make-up than I usually put on.

I checked my watch. Just after ten.

Kirsty Wickens! For God's sake, I was meant to be finding out the circumstances of Humphrey Carter's death, not sitting around snivelling. She'd said I could ring between ten and twelve.

Kirsty sounded glad to get my call. Was there any chance we could meet? As soon as possible.

I was at least as keen as she was. I said I could do that morning, depending on her commitments.

Turned out she lived in East Sheen. And I'd have to go to her place because one of the kids was off school with some bug.

I said I'd be there in as long as it took and set out to navigate the public transport links of South London.

FOURTEEN

It's a fiddly journey from Herne Hill to Mortlake. Maybe it's quicker by bus but reading on buses gives me a headache, so I always prefer trains. Herne Hill to Victoria. Clapham Junction to Mortlake.

The train had stopped at Putney when my mobile rang. The display told me it was Dodge. Which, as I said, was unusual. He rarely rang me.

'Hello?'

'Ellen, I've finished some more wood.' His voice was, as ever, incongruously upper class.

'Sorry? *Finished*? What do you mean?'

'Some more of the good wood. I've sanded it down and prepared it for use.'

'Ah. Yes. Fine.' I was distracted and couldn't think what relevance this information might have for me. 'Congratulations.'

'I was lucky with the weather. Cold but not raining. So, I could do the sanding and stuff on the workbench outside.'

'Ye–es.' I was still confused.

'Which, I'm pretty sure, means he saw me doing it.'

'*He*?'

'The thief.'

'Ah.' Belatedly, I was up to speed with what he was talking about.

'So, Ellen, would this evening be all right for you?'

I was lost again. 'All right for what?'

'For trying to capture the thief.'

'Should be OK. I'm in London right now. I'll call you when I get back to Chi.'

'Thanks, Ellen. I'm determined to get him.' The way Dodge said it, he didn't sound vindictive. More intrigued, I'd say.

East Sheen is between Barnes and Richmond. Though not quite having the cachet of either, property prices there are almost as high. A lot of media people live along that strip south of the Thames. It's also a factory farm for the production of babies. Aspirational young couples settle there to start breeding, before moving to the outer suburbs when they run out of space. The Waitrose is full of buggies.

The Wickens' house was a semi, probably Edwardian in origin, with pebble-dashed frontage. In a road where a lot of refurbishment and making-over had taken place, it looked marginally shabby, with evidence of cracked paint on the window frames. And the sitting room, into which Kirsty ushered me, could also have done with a lick of paint.

Of course, because she had been behind the camera filming the birthday lunch, this was the first time I'd seen Humph and Theresa's younger daughter. She didn't have the striking looks of her sister. In fact, she seemed to have inherited few of her parents' best features. Her father's height made her look gawky and, on her, the natural blonde of the younger Theresa Carter had come out mousy. Bearing two children had left her thick around the waist. The sweatshirt and leggings she wore didn't add much to the overall impression.

Maybe, I thought, her very dowdiness was one of the reasons why she had been her father's favourite daughter. Less competition.

There was a great weariness about Kirsty's blue eyes. Maybe it was just the stresses of motherhood, staying up at night with a sick child, but I detected signs of deeper emotional strain. I was struck by the thought that, of all those close to the late Humphrey Carter, Kirsty was the one to whom his death had caused most grief. Theresa's poised exterior made it impossible to know how much she was suffering underneath. Chloe had been glad to see the back of her father. But the younger daughter was clearly a victim of sudden bereavement. I got the feeling it would take her a long time to recover.

The sitting room was untidy – though not on a scale to offer a challenge to SpaceWoman. It simply bore witness to that untidiness that comes with having two small children in the house. I remembered it well, that inability ever to get the last toy or scrap of crayoned paper out of the way before the next avalanche arrived.

'Can I get you a coffee or something?' asked Kirsty.

'No, I'm fine.'

'Well, do sit down.'

I sank more deeply than I'd expected into a sofa which had been loved almost to the point of dilapidation. Kirsty moved an open laptop from an armchair so that she could sit in it. 'Sorry, just doing a bit of work.'

'Can I ask what you do?'

'Of course. Copyediting manuscripts for publishers. I was an editor before I had the kids, and the theory is that I can do this around their demands.' She didn't make it sound as if the juggling job was an easy one.

'Oh, I should have asked, Kirsty. How is the one who's sick?'

'Not too bad. Streaming cold, bit of a temperature. One of those bugs which has been going round the school and which the rest of the family will no doubt catch very soon.' She spoke with that archetypal mother's weariness.

Then she seemed to pick herself up and remember her manners. 'It's very good of you to come all this way. I think Mum said you were based in Chichester – is that right?'

'Yes, but I was in London last night, so it's no great sweat.'

'No.' She looked at her watch, a trifle nervously. I remembered how specific her text had been about my ringing between ten and twelve. What was going to happen at twelve that she was worried about?

'You know that I have seen the video you took of your father's birthday lunch?'

'Yes. Mum told me.'

'Which is rather strange. Because it means I know what other members of your family look like, but I'm seeing you for the first time. I didn't get your kids' names, by the way . . . ?'

'Justin and Molly.'

'How old?'

'Justin's eight and Molly six.'

'Which one's the invalid?'

'Molly. Always a bit of a drama queen, not one to make light of her illness.'

'I know the syndrome,' I said. Not because that had been particularly true of either of my children, but I wanted to make

myself part of the freemasonry of mothers, empathize to put
Kirsty Wickens at her ease. 'And I gathered from the video,' I
went on, 'that the kids adored their grandfather.'

'Yes.' She was suddenly struck by emotion, almost choking
as she continued. 'I don't think they've taken it in yet, that they
won't see him again. I really haven't worked out the best way
to help them take it on board. Would going to the funeral help?
Would that bring some kind of closure to them? I just don't
know.'

'What does your husband think?'

'What – Garth?' Her dismissive tone showed how much she
valued his input. Then she tried to backtrack. 'Well, obviously
we've discussed it, but neither of us can make up our minds.'

'I gather he's a writer, your husband?'

'Yes. Used to be in publishing, that's where we met. But then
he lost his job and . . . thought he'd try writing.'

'Gamekeeper turned poacher?' I suggested.

'If you like.'

'Does he work from home?'

'No, he takes his laptop out to a café in the park and writes
there.'

'Like J.K. Rowling?' I suggested.

'I wish. God, if we had one per cent of her royalties . . . No,
Garth says he finds it easier to concentrate with people around
him. That's where he is now.' She didn't seem keen to dwell on
the subject of Garth Wickens. I didn't pursue it. I remembered
the cruelty of his father-in-law's comments at the birthday lunch.
Garth may have called himself a writer, but he remained an
unpublished writer.

'You mentioned the funeral, Kirsty. Has that been sorted? Has
a date been set?'

'Provisional. Just a few details that Mum needs to sort out
with the police, then they'll confirm when the inquest is to take
place. Once that's done, then they'll . . . release the body.'
Again, the reality of her father's death threatened her
equilibrium.

'Theresa suggested to me there'd be a small private funeral.'

'Yes,' Kirsty agreed. 'And then a big memorial service in London
at some point. Humph was a major figure in the entertainment

business, you know. Lots of celebs would want to be there to raise a glass to him.'

I couldn't judge how accurate that was. Chloe hadn't thought such a memorial service would be well attended. So, I just said, 'Yes.'

'He did interview just about anyone who was anyone back then.'

Yes, 'back then', I thought, aware of the short shelf life of television celebrity. I remembered Niall Fitzpatrick quoting the broadcasting executive, 'Who knows or cares who Sammy Davis Junior and Jerry Lewis were? Come to that, who knows or cares who John Smith and Robin Cook were?'

'He was brilliant,' Kirsty went on. 'I've been playing back a lot of the *Humphrey Carter Interviews* . . . My father did have an amazing talent.'

I hadn't seen enough of his work to comment. 'What?' I asked, 'you've got videos of all the old shows, have you?'

'I've had them digitized. So, I can watch them on the laptop . . . whenever I want to.'

There was a catch in her voice. I had a sudden image of her sitting alone watching her father's old shows, perhaps feeling a desperately needed closeness to the deceased. It reinforced my view that she was the one whom the death had hit hardest.

Kirsty hesitated. It was clear she wanted to get on to more controversial ground but didn't know how to do it. I tried to ease the way for her. 'You've presumably heard from your mother the suspicions she has about Humph's death?'

'Yes. Yes, I have. That's why I was surprised to hear from her that the police are talking about releasing the body after the inquest.'

'Because that would mean they're expecting – and accepting – the suicide verdict?'

'Yes.'

'Do I detect that you share your mother's doubts?'

'You do. I just can't believe that Humph would ever kill himself. He was such a life force. He would never take the coward's way out.' She was passionate in her father's defence. I bit back my reaction to her choice of words. In my mind, suicide could never be linked to cowardice.

'Do you buy the possibility that the death could have been an accident?' I asked cautiously. I wasn't going to be the one to mention the *M* word.

Kirsty shook her head firmly. 'It couldn't have been. Not with the sleeping pills crushed into the whisky bottle. Somebody did that deliberately. Humph was murdered.' All right. She'd said it. 'That's what Mum suggested to you, wasn't it?'

I nodded.

'She told me that you agreed with her . . .'

'Well . . .'

'. . . and that you were, kind of, investigating the case.'

'I'm . . . let's say I'm checking out some of the evidence.'

'All right.'

My next question was the obvious one. 'So, Kirsty, who do you think did it?'

She didn't answer directly. She said, 'Did you know that my parents have got a flat in Covent Garden?'

'I had heard that, yes.'

'There was a stage when I was at uni in London, and I used to use it occasionally.'

'OK,' I said, wondering where this was going.

'I had a set of keys.'

'Right.'

'I never stayed overnight because I had student accommodation in Kilburn but sometimes, you know, if I'd got a gap between lectures, I might nip into the flat to cook myself a bowl of pasta, something like that.'

Various possibilities were forming in my head as to what she might say next, but I offered no prompt.

Not that she needed one. 'One afternoon I went to the flat and found Humph there. He wasn't alone.'

'Ah. What did he say to you?'

'He didn't say anything. He'd got music on in the bedroom and he didn't hear my key in the lock. I just saw them through the crack in the bedroom door and then let myself out quietly. Humph never knew I'd been there. Do you want to know who he was with?'

I wasn't that bothered, but I said, 'Yes.' The name of one of his cub reporters or television researchers wouldn't mean anything to me.

'Have you heard of an actress called Zena Fitzpatrick?' she asked.

Surprised by the direction the conversation was going, I said that I had. 'She was married to Niall, who was at the birthday lunch, isn't that right?'

'Yes. Humph had a long affair with her.' Kirsty sounded almost proud of her father's actions. She certainly wasn't condemning them.

I was a bit puzzled. Niall had told me that Humph and Zena had always met at anonymous London hotels. Never at the Covent Garden flat. Still, maybe Kirsty had witnessed them together at a very early stage of their liaison, or on a day when logistical problems had prevented them from using their customary caution.

I wondered whether I should tell her that I'd already had some of this information from Niall but decided not to. 'Did your mother know about the affair?' I asked.

Kirsty shook her head. 'I genuinely don't think she did. Zena was one of her best friends, had been since they were both at RADA together. I certainly never mentioned anything to her about it. No, I don't think she did know.'

'And you don't think she found out about the affair after Zena died?'

'Why do you ask that?'

'Well, to put it bluntly, Kirsty, if Theresa did find out about an affair that had gone on behind her back for so long between two people she thought she could trust . . . then she would have had a motive to murder Humph.'

'Oh, no!' She didn't like that idea. 'Mum always loved him.'

'OK. But, if we're going down this route, we have a very narrow list of suspects. Accepting that Theresa didn't kill him, then who did?'

'I think Niall did it.'

'Why?'

'Out of jealousy. After Zena died, he must have found something when he went through her belongings. I don't know, a diary, some letters . . . something that revealed the truth of her long-term affair with his friend and work colleague. That pushed him over the edge and the only revenge possible to him was to murder Humph.'

I was about to tell her the unlikeliness of the scenario she had just spelled out. I had been told by Niall Fitzpatrick that he'd known about his wife's affair for more than thirty years. If his motive was jealousy or revenge, why would he have waited till after his wife's death to take action?

But I didn't get a chance to say any of that. There was the sound of the front door opening. Kirsty looked with panic at her watch as her husband walked into the room.

She introduced me, not mentioning that I was the one who found her father's body. But her husband would have known that.

Garth Wickens didn't seem interested in me, anyway. 'What's for lunch?' he asked.

'I'll sort it out in a moment,' she said. 'Do you want to go up and see how Molly is?'

'Not particularly,' said Garth, sitting down in an armchair and placing a laptop on the floor beside him.

As if hearing her cue – or perhaps wakened by the sound of the front door – a wail was heard from the invalid upstairs. Kirsty looked fiercely at her husband, willing him to take action. But all he did was say, 'You'd better go and sort her out.'

Seething, Kirsty stumped up the stairs.

'I gather you're a writer, Garth,' I said, trying to fill the silence.

'You have it in one,' he replied.

'A good morning on the book?'

'I'm making headway,' he said gnomically.

'Can I ask what kind of book you're writing?'

'No,' he replied. Then, realizing that he was being unnecessarily rude, 'I'm sorry. I'm superstitious when it comes to talking about work in progress.'

'Probably very sensible.'

Silence reasserted itself. Then Garth said, 'And you're the one who found Humph's body . . . ?'

'Yes.'

'Must have been a shock for you.'

'It was.'

'Typical Humph, that was. Topping himself. Flamboyant to the end.'

I might have questioned his certainty about the suicide conclusion, had not Kirsty reappeared. 'Wants some hot Ribena,' she said.

'Your friend was just asking me how the book's going,' said Garth.

'Oh yes?' She looked at me. 'And what did you find out, Ellen? He never tells me anything.'

'Apparently, all going fine,' I said.

'Yes,' Garth agreed. He addressed his next remark directly to his wife, for whom the words seemed to have some secret marital resonance. 'I'm finding it much easier to concentrate now your father's dead.'

The look on Kirsty Wickens' face told me everything. She had tried to blame Niall Fitzpatrick for the crime because she was afraid that it was her husband who had murdered Humphrey Carter.

It was a dark night. Cold, too. We didn't have the heater on in the Yeti because Dodge was afraid of engine noise betraying our hiding place. He'd parked the 1951 Morris Commer CV9/40 Tipper van back outside my house and, as per agreement, I'd driven him back to his.

Dodge was very confident about what was going to happen, as self-assertive as I'd ever seen him. He repeated that he felt sure he'd been under observation when he was working on the wood outside in his yard. He also reckoned that the thief would have clocked the departure of the Commer van early in the evening and taken that as his cue to perform the snatch.

I didn't share this certainty. I thought Dodge's assumptions were based on insufficient evidence about his tormentor. But I didn't say that. I cherished the moments when Dodge actually asked me to do something for him. They were rare and I thought they maybe strengthened the fragile bond between us. With the possibility of Ben being permanently off my radar, I would need all the friends I could get.

The road off which Dodge's property lies is quite rural, leading out of Walberton towards a couple of working farms and more farmhouses converted into upmarket dwellings for retired city-dwellers, who regard the country as a kind of adventure playground. The track is narrow and potholed. There's a wooded area either side of Dodge's entrance and that was where we were hidden. A few cars came past during our vigil, but none turned in.

We didn't talk much in the cold Yeti. Dodge and I never did talk much, but I'd long since stopped feeling any awkwardness about that state of affairs. I've always thought the ability to be silent with someone is a measure of a relationship's strength rather than its weakness.

But, as the cold bit into my bones, the silence allowed other thoughts to invade my mind. Disquieting thoughts about the murder of Humphrey Carter. More worrying than those, thoughts about my son and daughter. And where I had gone wrong in my relationships with both of them.

Accompanying those thoughts came the old, inevitable, enduring pang. How much I wanted to discuss the various situations with Oliver.

Maybe I dozed. Certainly, Dodge's tapping on my arm gave me an unexpected jolt. I opened my eyes to see a pair of tail-lights disappearing through the open gate into his yard.

'Do you want to catch him in the act?' I whispered.

'No. I want to see where he takes the wood.'

'OK,' I said. Though I didn't really think it was OK. Lack of sleep the previous night and the stresses of the morning were catching up with me. My agreement to help Dodge when he called me on the train had been instinctive, but I hadn't really thought through what it might entail.

Shutting off the exit from his property with the Yeti, perhaps, trapping the thief and catching him red-handed . . .? All I knew was that Dodge's plans wouldn't have included involving the police. This dispute would be settled between the victim of theft and the thief. What form that settlement would take I hadn't really considered.

Still, I wasn't keen on the idea of a night-time car chase through the West Sussex countryside. All I wanted was to be back home in Chichester as soon as was humanly possible.

But I had promised to help Dodge. And I knew, from previous dealings with him that, however illogical the process might sometimes seem, everything had to be done Dodge's way.

So, I waited dutifully.

It took the thief over half an hour to do the job . . . presumably to open the house, take all the newly finished wood from its first floor store to his van, and drive back out on to the road.

I hadn't seen which direction he'd come from, but I assumed he was going back the same way.

Again, Dodge knew exactly what he was doing. He told me not to start the Yeti until the other van was a couple of hundred yards away and not to switch on my headlights. There was no roadside illumination or anything reflecting from the farm buildings we passed, so it was quite possible our quarry didn't know he was being followed.

The visibility changed when he took a turn on to the A27 going towards Fontwell. But, as well as more light, there was more traffic, so the Yeti's surveillance role was less obvious. I switched the headlights on as soon as we joined the main road. Didn't want to draw attention to ourselves and be stopped by the police.

'I thought it was,' said Dodge, who could now see the detail of the vehicle we were tracking.

'What?' I asked. So far as I knew, it was just an old van, open at the back. A couple of propped-up planks of wood were visible over the edge.

'1972 Ford Transit Mk1 Pick-Up,' said Dodge. Then, with a note of admiration, 'It's been very well looked after.'

Our quarry didn't stay long on the A27. Turned off soon after the Fontwell roundabout towards Eartham, but then got involved in a network of minor roads and farm tracks. Dodge knew the area well enough not to worry about losing contact. He directed me to drive out of sight of the van ahead, but with such conviction that I wondered if he'd done a recce on the location, maybe had some inside knowledge of where the thief lived.

He certainly let out a sigh of satisfaction as he told me to stop the Yeti, with its headlights off again, outside a farm entrance whose open gates slumped despairingly into clumps of nettles.

'This is it,' he said, pointing up the overgrown drive to where the Transit was just visible, parked in front of an unlit, broken-backed house. 'Is he going to unload the stuff straight away?'

The answer seemed to be no. We could just about discern the outline of a short, puffa-jacketed figure getting out of the Transit and disappearing round the side of the house.

This time Dodge instructed me to park across the entrance, so that our target couldn't escape that way. Then he led me to the back of the house. The sky was still moonless but, the more time we spent in the dark, the better we could detect the outlines of the buildings around us.

As we rounded the edge of the house, we saw some light. Coming from a dilapidated caravan. Not a caravan in romantic gypsy style, just a stained metal box whose designer had taken inspiration from sardine tins. Its tyres had long since deflated and the wheelrims rose up from a tangle of weeds.

Dodge seemed more confident than ever. With me hurrying in his wake, he strode on long legs up to the caravan's door and rapped on it sharply.

The owner was unlikely to be expecting anyone at that time of night but, having just put the lights on, couldn't pretend they weren't there.

The door opened to reveal a short, combative woman with blue hair, whose arms were a gallery of tattoos. 'What do you want?' she demanded aggressively.

But Dodge wasn't looking at her. His eyes went beyond, to the interior. As in some kind of strange Tardis, in incongruous contrast to the caravan's grimy shell, the inside walls were in the process of being panelled in beautiful wood.

'God,' murmured Dodge. 'That's amazing!

FIFTEEN

By Dodge's standards, he was quite garrulous on the way back to my place. Which means that he spoke two sentences without my prompting him. And both sentences covered pretty much the same ground.

'That Mazz,' he said (Mazz was what the blue-haired girl called herself), 'she really knows how to work with wood.'

'She also,' I pointed out, 'knows how to steal it.'

He didn't respond to that. I drove on in silence. There hadn't been much conversation in the caravan, either. No point in Dodge asking Mazz whether it was she who'd been stealing his wood. The evidence was on the caravan walls and in the back of her Transit van.

She recognized him. Hardly surprising, since she'd been keeping him under surveillance to know when the next load of wood was ready for stealing. Though, of course, she didn't know his name.

She made no apologies for her thieving, and Dodge didn't berate her for it either. He just said, rather awkwardly, 'I'll have to see what I do about this.'

'You won't go to the police?' the girl had pleaded. If she'd known Dodge as well as I do, she wouldn't have needed to ask the question. There was something strange about her manner, a mixture of the feral, the belligerent and the vulnerable. What she had said suggested that her occupation of the caravan wasn't strictly legal.

'No,' Dodge had replied. 'It won't be police.'

'What will it be then?'

'I'll have to think about that,' he mumbled. At no point during their encounter had his eyes met the girl's.

He suggested that the next step would be for them to exchange phone numbers. My first thought, that someone apparently living wild wouldn't have a mobile, was quickly dashed. Everyone, even those living on the streets, has a mobile now.

And that was it. Mazz, still anxious, again asked Dodge what he was going to do. He didn't answer her question, just said that it was time for us to go. And that he'd be in touch.

As we left, the girl looked paranoid.

When we got back to mine, I invited Dodge in for a drink, hoping he'd decline. He did, bless him. He always did, but often my invitation was more heartfelt than this one. The fact was that I hadn't really warmed up properly after our chilly surveillance session. All I wanted at that moment was a glass of Merlot, on my own, and quickly to bed with an extra duvet and a hot water bottle. The day was catching up on me.

As we got out of the Yeti, and Dodge started towards his 1951 Morris Commer CV9/40 Tipper van, he said again, 'She really knows how to work with wood.'

Jools wasn't at home that night. Or the next one. She didn't contact me. Either things were going very well in Worthing or . . . I didn't like to think about the 'or' . . . I didn't like to think about where I stood with Ben either. I tried to focus solely on what needed doing for SpaceWoman.

It was a couple of days later I had a call from Theresa Carter to tell me that the inquest on Humphrey Carter had just taken place. 'I wanted you to know as quickly as possible, in case the press got on to you.'

'What was the verdict?'

'Suicide. Like the police said it would be.'

'And has that changed your views?'

'No.'

'Hm.' I wasn't sure whether that was the answer I wanted. Probably yes. My curiosity about the true circumstances of Humphrey Carter's death was now so intense that I too would have been disappointed to accept the suicide verdict.

'Anyway, Theresa, why do you think the press would be on to me?'

'Oh, come on, Ellen. Who found the body?'

'I take your point.'

'Look, I've literally just come out of the court. Humph's agents – the television and literary ones – are with me. They've managed to control the coverage so far, but now the verdict's official, there'll be a media frenzy. Nothing we can do to stop it. But I just wanted to say, Ellen, that it's not going to be helpful for us to express our real views on the subject.'

'You mean, if asked, we pretend to accept the suicide verdict?'

'We have to.'

'Forever?'

'I don't know,' she said, her voice flat with exhaustion. 'All I do know is that I'm bone-deep weary. I haven't got the energy to fight any more. The official records will say that Humph's death was by suicide. It won't be the first time official records have got things wrong. Does it really matter?'

At the end of the phone call, I felt frustrated. I didn't realize how deeply the investigation had embedded itself in me. I couldn't just abandon it with so many loose ends left hanging.

It might not matter to Theresa Carter. But it still mattered to me.

I was glad she'd warned me, because the minute I'd ended the call, my phone rang. *'Daily Mail'*, female reporter. Had heard that I was the person who had discovered Humphrey Carter's body. She was writing a feature on showbiz suicides. Mentioned the names of Kurt Cobain, Robin Williams, Caroline Flack. Had I realized as soon as I saw the body that—?

I cut the call off. But the phone kept ringing. I checked the numbers. None of them did I recognize. So, I didn't answer any of them.

Then came the ringing of my doorbell. Unthinking, I opened the door to the first one. I hadn't realized till then that putting 'a foot in the door' was a real thing. I like to think he limped away after I'd slammed it on him.

With the media circus camped on my doorstep, I got on the phone and cancelled my SpaceWoman appointments for the day. There was no way I was going to run the gauntlet of reporters. Instead, I would occupy myself with the long overdue task of doing the company accounts. This was not a part of being a small business that I enjoyed, but my accountant kept on at me about the imperative of keeping the books up to date. So, here was a heaven-sent opportunity to get the boring stuff done.

I had to give the press full marks for persistence. They didn't stop phoning. They didn't stop ringing my doorbell. I even found doing my accounts a welcome distraction.

'What the hell's going on out there?' demanded Jools, as she let herself in early afternoon. She was wearing her SpaceWoman livery of logoed blue polo shirt and leggings. Since I'd last seen her wearing a dress, this meant she'd been back to Chichester from Worthing while I'd been away.

'What is going on,' I replied, 'is a media furore, following the announcement of a suicide verdict on Humphrey Carter.'

'Ah,' she said. 'Yes, there's been a lot about it on social media.'

'I'm sure there has.'

'Haven't you looked?' I shook my head. 'You're mentioned by name.'

That gave me yet another reason to avoid social media except for strictly decluttering purposes. But I didn't mention that to my daughter. She already thought I was sufficient of a dinosaur.

I needed a break. Constantly moving my head between invoices and the Excel spreadsheet had given me the beginnings of a headache. 'Fancy a coffee?' I asked.

'Yes.' Jools's reply was cautious. She did want a cup of coffee, but she didn't want to get involved in talking about anything serious. I also wanted a cup of coffee, but I did want to get involved in talking about something serious.

As we moved through to the kitchen, the landline rang. I went straight to the coffee machine.

'Aren't you going to answer it?' asked Jools.

I looked at the display. 'Not a number I recognize. More press.'

'Ah. You're going to have to talk to them at some point, Mum.'

'Why?'

'Otherwise, they'll think you're hiding something. Lots of conspiracy theorists online, you know.'

'I'm sure there are.'

'"Suicide Mystery of Showbiz Legend". They'll love that.'

'I'm sure they will.'

'It'll be a True Crime podcast in no time.'

'I've a horrible feeling that's true.' Change of subject. 'How are things in Worthing?'

'Fine.' Clearly all I was going to get.

I handed across her coffee and sat at the kitchen table. The offer was implicit. Jools hesitated for a moment before sitting down opposite me.

'You know I saw Ben a few days back.'

'I knew you were going to, but I'd forgotten.'

She didn't ask me for any more information, so I didn't give any. There had been times when Ben and Jools had got on pretty well, but they were basically very different characters. For her to show no interest in what he was doing was not unusual. And, given my complicated feelings about my son, it wasn't the moment for me to volunteer anything about the lunch.

'The night after seeing him,' I said, 'I stayed in the flat.'

'Ah,' said Jools. It was a monosyllable loaded with complex thoughts.

'Of course, I checked that everything was all right there. A bit dusty, but no major problems. There weren't any leaks from the plumbing, nothing like that.' I was conscious of the cumbersome way I was getting round to what I wanted to say.

Jools was silent. She had the wary look of a cat, ready to leap away at any sudden movement.

No point in further delaying tactics. Just go for it. 'I met Mr Driscoll.'

'Ah.' This one was carrying even more freight.

'Well, I say I met him. I saw him. I tried to meet him.'

'That sounds more likely,' said my daughter drily.

'Jools, I have to know what your relationship is with him!'

'Why?'

'Because men of his age don't give a lot of money to young women for no reason.'

'I see.' She was silent for a moment. 'So, what do you think our relationship is?'

'I don't know. Otherwise, I wouldn't be asking, would I?'

'But I dare say your imagination has been working overtime?'

'Maybe. That's what imaginations do when they have no actual facts to go on.'

'So, in which direction has your imagination been going this time?'

'Well, there is quite a common phenomenon these days,' I foundered, 'with the cost of living crisis . . . whereby young women get helped to pay for their accommodation by . . . by providing older men with . . . certain services . . .'

She twigged. 'You mean you think I've been having sex with him?'

'Well, I—'

'God, Mum, what do you take me for?' The disgust was visible in her face. 'Do you think I have no standards at all?'

'I just don't know, Jools,' I said wretchedly.

She stood up, giving me a look of total contempt. Before she went up to her room, I got an acid, 'Thank you for the coffee.'

But she'd hardly touched it.

I hadn't thought to listen to the news at lunchtime, but I watched the BBC's six o'clock bulletin. By then the phoning journalists and those camped outside my house had finally got the message that they weren't going to get anything out of me.

There wasn't a lot about Humph on the news. As usual, international conflicts and bombings and people generally destroying each other got the lion's share of the coverage. Also, the death of Humphrey Carter had already been covered when it happened. In the days afterwards, there were a few tributes from people in the television industry. Younger talk show hosts, who thought they did the job much better than he had done, were fulsome in their praise, saying how Humph had taught them everything they knew. A couple of his former interviewees were wheeled out to pronounce showbiz platitudes about the shows being 'just like chatting with an old friend'.

Humph himself would, I'm sure, have wanted more, but television memories are short.

So, although it might be thought to be more newsworthy than the announcement of an eighty-year-old's death, the fact that he had committed suicide got only a passing mention. And it was immediately backed up by a clip from a television psychologist saying how harmful social media was in encouraging suicidal thoughts in young people. This comment, though undoubtedly true, had absolutely no relevance to Humphrey Carter's death.

A day of my mobile constantly ringing and me not picking up made me think of Perry Driscoll. It was so easy now all phones had number displays. Check who it is ringing and then decide whether you want to talk to them or not. Did Perry Driscoll ever want to talk to anyone? Probably not.

Or did he perhaps have a list of numbers he would talk to? A very short list, I reckoned. And then the chilling thought came to me that my daughter might be on that list.

I'd tried phoning him. I'd tried talking to him face to face. The one means of contact I hadn't tried was email. And, of course, Mehmet from the Kalkan Kaffee had given me his address. I looked at it. The username was *Cheeryble*, which rang a distant bell for me, but I couldn't put my finger on where I'd heard it.

I spent a long time framing my message. I was aware that Jools was in the house. Still in her room. More like a grumpy teenager than a grown woman in her twenties.

After many false starts, I came up with a formula of words with which to address Perry Driscoll. I knew it was extremely unlikely to elicit a response from him, but I had to try. This is what I came up with:

> Dear Mr Driscoll, (I didn't really think 'Hi' was appropriate for this kind of communication.)
>
> I am Ellen Curtis, the mother of Jools who owns the flat underneath yours. We met a few days ago when I spoke to you in the Kalkan Kaffee. I apologize that I took you by surprise and caused you to leave the premises. It was certainly not my intention to distress you.
>
> I gather from my daughter that she confided in you about some financial problems she was having, and you were generous enough to help her by paying some of her bills while she got over that sticky patch. I also gather that you are continuing to meet various expenses for her, including her mortgage repayments. Because I do not like the idea of my daughter being in debt to anyone, I would be most grateful if you could let me know why you are showing her such generosity.
>
> (I gave him my mobile number and rounded off the message) All good wishes, Ellen Curtis.

It sounded horribly formal, and I considered it was most unlikely to prompt any reaction. But I couldn't think of anything else to do, so I sent it off to him.

SIXTEEN

I had been worried that I'd wake up the following morning to a further barrage of phone calls and more reporters camped in my front garden. But all was mercifully quiet. Humphrey Carter's suicide was yesterday's story and media interest had moved on to a verbal gaffe perpetrated by a junior royal.

I did, however, look online for coverage. In most of the papers, this took the form of features on famous suicides, artists in various media who had taken their own lives. Humph might have been flattered to be listed alongside Vincent Van Gogh, Mark Rothko, Ernest Hemingway, Virginia Woolf, Sylvia Plath, Michael Hutchence and Kurt Cobain. Though he wouldn't have been so pleased by the commentators' snide suggestions that he didn't really belong in such exalted company.

Some papers just used the death as a springboard for another piece about the dangers of suicide among young men (something of which, having lived so long with Ben, I was all too aware).

Basically, Humphrey Carter himself got lost in all the column inches. He would have been very pissed off.

Jools had left the house before I got up that morning. There was a note on the kitchen table, saying that she was off doing a recce on a house in Shoreham, whose owner suffered from obsessive Ocado grocery ordering. While I was glad that my daughter was generating SpaceWoman work on her own initiative – something I'd been encouraging her to do – I still felt her early start was just a way of avoiding me.

Having not done much SpaceWoman work outside the house in the last week, I had to make a few rescheduling calls to organize my programme. Maybe I'd have time to drop in on Wanda Lyall before my first assignment . . .?

As I had this thought, my mobile rang. Kirsty Wickens.

'So, it's official,' she announced. 'My father killed himself. Except he didn't.'

'You're still convinced he was murdered?'

'More than ever. Aren't you, Ellen?'

Rather unwillingly, I had to admit that I was.

'Well, in a way,' said Kirsty, 'this makes our job easier.'

'Our job being the unmasking of the perpetrator?'

'Of course.'

'I don't quite see how the inquest verdict makes it easier.'

'Because, Ellen, the police are no longer involved. That means they won't get in our way.'

I didn't quite follow her logic, but I wasn't about to challenge it.

'Since I heard the news,' she went on, 'I've been going through some of Humph's stuff that Mum passed on to me.'

'What kind of stuff?'

'Oh, the diaries, you know.'

'I remember, Kirsty, when Theresa mentioned those to me, she said there were one or two appointments just marked by initials. Did you come across any of those?'

'Yes, most of the regular ones I kind of worked out. *PPM* I reckon was Programme Planning Meeting. *GL*– probably Garrick Lunch. A few I could guess at. But there was one *SE* . . . I had no idea what that meant.'

'Do you think maybe—?'

But she cut across me. 'More importantly, Ellen, I've been looking through the old *Humphrey Carter Interviews* . . . recordings.'

I was tempted to ask why, but fortunately she answered the question for me. 'I was wondering whether there was someone Humph offended in one of the interviews, someone who might have had a grudge against him.'

Knowing his abrasive reputation, I had no doubt there were many guests he had rubbed up the wrong way. He certainly claimed that offended politicians had kept his name off the Honours List. But to my mind, the circumstances of his death made it almost impossible that the murderer was someone who hadn't been sitting round that birthday lunch table. The idea of an outsider infiltrating Staddles, creeping up to Humph's study to adulterate the Famous Grouse bottle with crushed-up sleeping pills . . . well, it was just too incongruous to be true.

But I didn't say any of that to Kirsty. I just asked, 'Has your opinion changed then? Is Niall no longer your chief suspect?'

'I think he probably still is, but I'm just checking out other possibilities. Oh, I'm so frustrated!' she said suddenly. 'Humph's dead and I know he was murdered. There's no way he would have killed himself. He loved me too much to do anything like that.'

I could see exactly the form her grief was taking. And I could share her frustration. Action was needed but it was difficult to know what that action should be.

I had a thought. 'You said you'd digitized the *Humphrey Carter Interviews* . . . recordings?'

'That's right. I'm going to want to watch them lots of times in the future. I know I will. To, sort of, keep Humph alive.'

'I wonder . . . would you mind sending copies to me? You know, an outside eye might see something in them that you're too involved to notice.'

She liked the idea. 'That'd be great. What's your email?'

I gave her the personal one, rather than SpaceWoman. Jools now had access to that, and I really didn't want to involve my daughter in the murder investigation. Kirsty said she'd send the recordings by WeTransfer. I asked if she had a list of the featured guests that she could send me as an email.

She had. It arrived moments after I'd finished our conversation. Among the yesterday's names of Sammy Davis Junior, Jerry Lewis, John Smith and Robin Cook, I noticed that Humphrey Carter had interviewed Zena Fitzpatrick. Now that was one I would like to have a look at.

But I couldn't watch it right then. I had to go off for the day's first SpaceWoman appointment. And, once again, I hadn't left time to go and see Wanda Lyall.

It was a routine job, one of those ongoing ones which involved weekly visits to check up on the hoarder. Again, one for which I hadn't invoiced since the initial clear-out. I was making too many calls like that. I haven't admitted to Jools how many. Though I probably ought to. Now we're both working for SpaceWoman, I shouldn't be keeping any secrets related to the business from her.

Again, that made me think about how our working relationship needed to be formalized. Was my daughter in with SpaceWoman for the long haul or not? Which prompted the other unrelated anxiety: what was there between her and Perry Driscoll? I hadn't had an email back from him. I hadn't really been expecting one.

When I got back in the Yeti after my visit, I saw there was a text from Theresa Carter. I rang her.

'Have the press stopped harassing you?' she asked straight away.

'Yes, fine now.'

'Did you give any interviews?'

'No, managed to avoid saying anything to any of them.'

'Congratulations.' There was a tone of weary relief in her voice.

'It must have been much worse for you.'

'Well, it would have been, but Humph's PR people brokered a deal.'

'How do you mean, Theresa?'

'Like a kind of buyout. I do an exclusive interview with the *Sunday Times* and the rest of them have to back off.'

'Ah. Have you done the interview yet?'

'No. Tomorrow morning. They're sending their *top interviewer* down to Staddles. I'd never heard of her. But I am rather dreading it.'

'I'm not surprised. But presumably you aren't planning to say anything controversial?'

'Like, for instance, that, in spite of the verdict, I still think Humph was murdered?'

'That was the kind of thing I had in mind, Theresa, yes.'

'No, I am not planning to do that.'

'Probably just as well.'

'Don't worry, Ellen. I know the correct way to behave. British Justice said it was suicide. I will not argue with British Justice.'

'Hm.'

'You don't sound convinced.'

'Don't I?'

'No, you sound like someone who still thinks Humph was murdered. And wants to continue investigating his death.'

'Do I?'

'Oh, for God's sake, let it rest, Ellen.'

'I don't think I can let it rest.'

There was a lot of exasperation in Theresa's sigh. 'So, where are your suspicions homing in now?'

'Not sure. Where would yours be, if you still had any suspicions?'

'You're something of a terrier, aren't you, Ellen?'

'Maybe.' It wasn't a description I found insulting.

To my surprise, Theresa said, 'All right, if you really want me to come up with some suspicions for your continuing investigation . . . I think I'd probably be wondering about Garth . . .'

'Oh? Why?'

'Well, there wasn't much love lost between the two of them. Humph was constantly needling him, going on about how he'd lost his job in publishing, how the Great Novel showed no signs of appearing, how Garth expected Kirsty to bring in all the family income. And, although I tried hard to like the man my daughter had chosen to marry, I'm afraid I came round to Humph's view. Garth really is a waste of space.'

'Yes, I've only met him briefly, but I wasn't impressed either. Still, if his father-in-law had always been badmouthing him, why should Garth suddenly decide to kill him on his eightieth birthday? Final straw breaking the camel's back?'

'Could be a bit of that. I think it's probably more likely Garth thought that, if Humph died, he and Kirsty might inherit something.'

'And will they?'

'No. Not till I pop my clogs. Our wills were very simple. Like lots of married couples, if one dies, everything goes to the survivor. Only when the survivor goes do the rest of the family get a look-in.'

'And Garth didn't know that?'

'He's quite stupid enough not to have taken it on board,' said Theresa, with some venom.

'Hm. Interesting.'

'You don't sound convinced, Ellen.'

'Well . . .'

'I'm not convinced myself. My mind's in such chaos at the

moment, I'm not really thinking straight.' There was a catch in her voice. Maybe another chink in her carapace of control? Was the shock of loss finally catching up with her?

But the moment quickly passed. She was all pragmatism as she went on, 'Anyway, thank God now I can stop constantly picking over my memories of Humph, looking for explanations.'

'Why can you stop?'

'Because, now we've got the coroner's verdict, I can move on to organizing the funeral.'

'Yes, of course. Just family, I gather?'

'And a few close friends. Niall will be there, of course. And I'd like you to come, Ellen.'

'Really? But I hardly knew Humph.'

'I'd like you to come, Ellen,' Theresa repeated firmly. 'Then you can report to me how your investigations are going.'

Later that day, to my considerable surprise, I received an email reply from Perry Driscoll. It read:

> Dear Mrs Curtis,
>
> Thank you for yours. I apologize for my rudeness to you in the Kalkan Kaffee. I am afraid I don't react well to surprises. Even if I know we have an arrangement to meet, I still get very nervous at the prospect of being in another person's company.
>
> Do not worry about the financial assistance I have been giving to your daughter. I am fortunate enough to be able to afford it without any effect on my personal lifestyle. But I would be horrified if you were to think that there was any sinister or ulterior motive in my actions.
>
> If you do wish to discuss this further, please understand that I do not like talking on the telephone and I do not welcome other people into my living accommodation. I would, however, agree, with some reluctance, to your meeting me in the Kalkan Kaffee, ON THE UNDERSTANDING THAT YOU GIVE ME NOTICE OF THE EXACT TIME YOU WILL BE ARRIVING.
>
> Perry Driscoll

Through my SpaceWoman work, I've got good at spotting the signs of various mental health conditions and straight away I was adding more to the profile I'd been building up of the email writer's personality.

When Jools came in that evening at the end of work, I showed her the reply I'd received.

She just said, 'Hm.'

That wasn't good enough for me. 'Jools, I have to ask you again – why did Perry Driscoll offer you the money?'

'I was in a bad place,' came the grumpy reply. 'About everything. I came into the house one day just as he was coming down from his flat. I was crying and he asked why. I told him some of the stuff.'

I wish you'd told me, I thought.

'And then I said that not having any money was making it all worse. And he said, "Well, that's something we can sort out." And he asked for my bank details and he started paying money into my account.'

'But didn't you feel guilty that he was doing that?'

'Mum, I was feeling so many things round then that I hadn't got any space in my brain for guilt.'

Again, I wished that my daughter had felt she could confide in me about her troubles. I wondered whether I would ever find out everything that had happened in the build-up to her trip to Budapest. I rather doubted it. And any details that did emerge would emerge very slowly.

'Well,' I said. 'I'm going to take up Perry Driscoll's offer. I will email him back and say that I'll see him in the Kalkan Kaffee at eleven o'clock tomorrow morning.'

The look Jools turned on me moved from annoyance to confusion, then from confusion to a kind of serenity.

'I'm going to come with you, Mum,' she said.

SEVENTEEN

My correspondence with Perry Driscoll continued on the same formal lines. I emailed:

> Dear Mr Driscoll, Thank you for yours. I would like to take up your offer of a meeting and suggest that I come to the Kalkan Kaffee at eleven o'clock tomorrow morning. (I specified the date because I didn't know how often he checked his In-Box.) I would be grateful if you could let me know whether this will be convenient for you.
>
> All good wishes,
> Ellen Curtis

I got a surprisingly prompt response. While making no pretence that he welcomed the encounter, Perry Driscoll said he would be waiting for me in the Kalkan Kaffee at eleven the following morning.

I didn't mention that Jools would be with me. While he might have relished meeting again the young woman whose lifestyle he had been funding for some months, there was also the possibility that her presence might, once again, frighten him off.

On the train up to London, I had my book and Jools had her phone. She was busy on it all the way from Chichester to Herne Hill. I was far too professional a mother to ask her what she was doing on it all that time, but I was intrigued.

I had learned my lesson from my children's television-watching habits in their early teens. Because of my dinosaur upbringing, I still thought of switching the set on to watch specific programmes, as listed in the *Radio Times*. I hadn't quite caught up with the constant remote-control-zapping through streaming options of the younger generation. And too many iterations of me saying 'What are you watching?' and Jools or Ben saying 'I don't know' had made me stop asking the question.

Jools's interactions on her mobile, however, did interest me. Another of the undiscussed causes of her breakdown had to do with her being trolled. Her aspirations to become an 'influencer' had been dashed by some unknown antagonists. And criticism of her looks had driven her to the extreme solution of having the botched nose-job in Budapest.

But there are some things a mother can't do. And shouldn't aspire to do. Monitoring her offspring's every action on a mobile phone is high up the list.

I tried to concentrate on my book.

'Good morning.'

Perry Driscoll looked up from his laptop as I took the seat opposite him. He checked the time on his watch. The dot of eleven confirmed (I know how obsessive recluses can be) 'Good morning.' he said.

Jools and I had agreed that I would go into Kalkan Kaffee first, alone. I'd walked briskly and she'd dawdled from the station. I had suggested the option of her going into her flat before she came to the café, but she rejected it. Maybe the place would prompt bad memories. The idea was, instead, that she would come in a few minutes later than me, order coffees for us at the counter and bring them to the table.

I had, unsurprisingly, thought a lot about how I'd approach this encounter. Knowing the hypersensitivity of types like Perry Driscoll, I would proceed with great caution. Certainly, no accusations or confrontation of any kind.

So, I started by saying, 'Mr Driscoll, I very much appreciate the generosity you have shown to my daughter.'

I saw immediately that he shared Dodge's inability to make eye contact with anyone. 'It's not important,' he mumbled. 'Money is not a problem.'

'It's a problem for many people,' I said. 'And very few are lucky enough to have a benefactor like you to help them out.'

Looking at him close to, balding, generally unprepossessing, the lurid suspicions I'd entertained about him being in a 'sex-for-rent' situation with my daughter seemed incongruous. And yet, at the same time if, against all likelihood, that should prove to be the case, the image became even more distressing.

'The money . . .' said Perry Driscoll, as if it were an annoying encumbrance, 'I inherited from my parents. Far more money than I could ever need. My outgoings are small. The flats I bought outright. The best thing the money did for me was to enable me to give up my job. It was not one I enjoyed.'

I was tempted to ask what he used to do, but I didn't want to interrupt the flow.

'So, how I spend the surplus of money that I have, I would have thought, is really up to me.'

'Good morning, Perry.'

I hadn't noticed Jools entering the Kalkan Kaffee. She put two cups of coffee down and sat next to me. I tensed. If he was going to do another runner, this would be the moment for it.

But . . . nothing. Perry seemed, if anything, to welcome Jools's presence. And he showed no signs of being surprised by it.

'All well?' he asked her. The words didn't sound natural to him, more like something he had learned. He had little experience of making normal conversation.

'I'm a lot better than I was when you last saw me, Perry,' Jools replied. 'And I want to say how grateful I am to you for helping me out when I was in a very bad place.'

He looked embarrassed by her gratitude. 'It wasn't a problem for me,' he said again. 'As I was just saying to . . . to your mother.' I don't think he'd forgotten my name. For some reason, he didn't feel comfortable saying it.

Strange, I thought, having this deeply personal conversation in a busy café. Mehmet kept calling out orders in Turkish to the kitchen, from where his daughter and the cooks shouted back. But we were on neutral ground where Perry Driscoll felt comfortable. That was the important thing.

'I've been thinking a lot about the situation,' said Jools. She sounded very grown-up and sensible. I was a little surprised. Unforgivably, it hadn't occurred to me that she would have come to the meeting with her own agenda.

'As I say, Perry, I greatly appreciate the help you gave me at a difficult time. But I think that you paying my bills has now got to stop.'

'Why? As I keep saying, the money is not a problem for me.'

'No, but it's becoming a problem for me.'

He looked bewildered by this idea. 'Why? I have given you the option of doing what I have done. To give up work, to spend your time doing whatever you want to do.'

'For a start, Perry,' she said, 'I do actually like work. I can now recognize that I had a major breakdown in the last few months. I wasn't behaving like myself. Now, I'm getting more sense of where I should be . . . though it's going to take a long time before I'm fully recovered.'

I listened in amazement and also, it has to be said, with some pain. Why couldn't my daughter be as articulate about the situation to her mother as she was being to this comparative stranger?

'So, what I would like you to do, Perry, is to stop the standing orders which are going into my account. I have to sort out my problems on my own. That may mean selling the flat.'

'I could buy it,' he said eagerly. 'Then, when I next have to move, I won't have to go so far.'

This might have sounded peculiar to someone with no knowledge of hoarding behaviour, but for me the outlines of Perry Driscoll's personality were becoming clearer by the minute.

'Or if I get some suitable work,' Jools went on, 'I might be able to keep the flat. Possibly get in tenants for a while but eventually move back in.'

What she said caused me only a slight pang. I knew the set-up of her working with me for SpaceWoman in Chichester could only be a temporary solution. More than pain, though, I felt pride at hearing my daughter sounding so positive.

Perry Driscoll was silent. More cheery Turkish shouts from the kitchen. Then I asked quietly, 'How many flats have you got?'

He shrugged. 'Four or five.'

'But you considered buying Jools's?'

'Just a sudden thought. If she's not selling, there goes that idea.'

'And presumably you don't have any tenants in any of them?' I asked.

'No.' He shuddered at the incongruity of the idea.

'And is it mostly Amazon orders you keep there?'

'You do get some very good bargains on Amazon.' His tone was eager, almost childlike.

'Hm,' I said. 'And do you do many acts of charity, like the one you've been doing for Jools?'

He looked uncomfortable. 'There are a few,' he mumbled.

'Is my daughter the first one who's asked you to stop?'

He nodded awkwardly.

'You do understand why she's saying that, don't you?' I asked.

'Not really. But it's up to her. If that's what she wants.'

'That's what I want,' said Jools.

I felt so proud of her. There were still a lot of details about her breakdown and its causes that need to be discussed, but I felt that a door to those conversations had been opened a chink.

'You said, Mr Driscoll . . .' He didn't suggest I should call him 'Perry'; the formality of our dealings was maintained. '. . . that the money you inherited enabled you to "spend your time doing whatever you want to do"?'

'Yes,' he agreed, with something like enthusiasm.

'And may I ask what it is that you want to do?'

'Of course,' he said. For the first time a nervous smile ventured on to his face, as he pointed at his laptop. 'I am reading the entire works of Dickens. And each time I get to the end, I start again at the beginning.'

As we walked back to Herne Hill station, I realized why his email address had sounded familiar. The Cheeryble Brothers were philanthropic twins in Charles Dickens's *Nicholas Nickleby*. That's where he must have got the name from. But they were less random in the application of their charity than Perry Driscoll.

The more I thought about him, the more neatly he fitted into the model of a particular type of hoarder. The fact that he would never let anyone into his flat suggested to me that it was so crammed with – possibly unopened – Amazon orders that there was no room inside. It was quite possible that there would only be a narrow passageway between the boxes which allowed him to access his bedroom and bathroom. The readiness with which he had pounced on the idea of buying Jools's flat probably meant even the space he still had in his own was threatened.

His talk of the other flats he owned but didn't rent out was unusual, but I reckoned I had the explanation for that too. Few hoarders were in the financial position to do what Perry Driscoll had done. I wouldn't have been at all surprised if each of those other flats was so crammed with stuff that he couldn't even enter them.

And like a hermit crab which, as every shell becomes too cramped, has to move on to another one, Perry would buy another flat. And so, the cycle repeated itself.

Of course, this was all only conjecture on my part, but I felt pretty sure my analysis was correct. I'd get Jools's views on the theory at some point, but this wasn't the moment.

Once again, in the train on the short hop to Victoria, I had my book and my daughter had her mobile.

At one point, I dared to start a conversation by saying, 'I was wondering, Jools, whether you—'

'Don't worry, Mum,' she said. 'I have a plan. I just haven't worked out all the details yet.'

Then, at Victoria, my daughter announced that she wasn't catching the same train as me. I was going back to Chichester. She was going to Worthing.

And I had to be content with that.

Not having known how long the encounter in Kalkan Kaffee was going to last, I'd cleared my SpaceWoman diary for the whole day, so when I got back to Chichester, I had some bonus time on my hands.

One thing I thought I really must do was to visit Wanda Lyall. I seemed to have put that off far too many times. Later in the day I'd go and see her. I meant to ring to fix a time, but somehow didn't get round to it.

At least, the situation between Jools and Perry Driscoll was clearer. Odd, but clearer. And, fortunately, not realizing my worst imaginings.

As for the situation with Ben and me . . . well, I closed my mind to it.

To keep my mind from straying back there, I concentrated on the matter of Humphrey Carter's death. My investigation, as I liked to think of it. And probably just mine, now that Theresa seemed to have lost interest in finding the truth. As I had the thought, it felt a bit harsh. Theresa had been through so much recently, maybe the inquest verdict had offered her an imperfect form of closure.

And, of course, I had something new to work on. From WeTransfer I could access all of Humph's old interviews, so carefully digitized by his younger daughter.

Kirsty had done a very good cataloguing job. She'd sent me an email list of all the interviews, with names of the guests and transmission dates. I didn't bother with the Sammy Davis Juniors, the Jerry Lewises, the John Smiths and the Robin Cooks. There was only one that interested me. Zena Fitzpatrick.

I checked the date. Yes, their affair had been going for some years when the recording happened. I was intrigued to see how they reacted to each other. They were both, of course, professional performers, practised in not giving away anything too personal. I wondered if the interview was, kind of, like a dare between them, a joke at the expense of the public – and their partners – later to be giggled over in bed.

The first thing that struck me when I started playing the interview, was how absolutely stunning Zena Fitzpatrick had been. I'd seen her on television and I'd seen the photographs in the house she'd shared with Niall, but to see her in relaxed close-up was something else again.

And she really did look relaxed. Whether that was because she was talking to her lover or just a demonstration of an actor's skill, I couldn't say. I could imagine men all over the country drooling and reflecting uncharitably on the shortcomings of their wives.

Humph himself looked striking too. His hair back then was black and not that over-intense dyed black one sees so often on television. He didn't have the beard. He looked large and imposing. I'm sure that, when he came on screen, quite a few of the disparaged female viewers were looking at their husbands with fresh contempt.

The event on which the interview was hung was the opening of a new television series in which Zena starred. The title didn't mean anything to me, but then there have been so many interchangeable television series over the years that that was hardly surprising. It was something historical, with Zena looking even more stunning as a Regency lady.

Humph's enthusiastic intro ran: 'And I welcome as our guest today one of the brightest and best of this country's acting talents.

She's delighted us on stage, television and film. Not only is she a great actress, she's also a great beauty. Will you please give an enormously warm welcome to . . . Zena Fitzpatrick!'

From there on, the interview followed conventional lines. Zena Fitzpatrick's background was discussed, her break into the theatre, her favourite roles, a few mildly bitchy anecdotes of other stars she had worked with.

They were both pros, and it showed. Skilfully, they varied the mood of the interview. A hilarious anecdote of some backstage mishap would be followed by a tribute to some recently deceased actor Zena had worked with. There were valuable insights into how she assessed a script she was offered, how she approached each new role, which parts she had most enjoyed playing, and which she still aspired to play.

It was an encounter between two experts at the top of their different games. The studio audience was loud in its applause when Humph signed off with the words, 'And thanks enormously to today's special guest – one of our most talented and beautiful actresses, a woman who can always bring something extra to every occasion – Zena Fitzpatrick! I'm Humphrey Carter. From both of us – goodbye!'

And yet, however professional the two of them had been, and however much Humphrey Carter vaunted himself as a serious journalist, what he had just produced was an hour of showbiz fluff. Not unenjoyable, not unskilful, just not of great significance to the average consumer of television.

To me, on the other hand, something I had heard in the show was of very great significance.

I went back to the recording of Humph's eightieth birthday lunch at Staddles.

And that confirmed to me that I had solved one of the major mysteries of the case.

I rang Kirsty. 'I think I've worked out the *SE* reference in the diaries.'

'Oh?'

'They're so regular. Meetings always in the afternoon. I think it must be a long-term love affair.'

'Yes. Mum wondered about that.'

'Well, you and I know who Humph was meeting, don't we?'

'Zena Fitzpatrick.'

'Exactly. The affair which Niall Fitzpatrick had always known about. He must have known the meaning of *SE* too.'

'But, Ellen, he never saw the diaries.'

'How do you know?'

'When Mum gave them to me, she said Humph had always kept them locked in his briefcase. She specifically said that Niall hadn't seen them.'

'He didn't need to have seen them to recognize the expression "something extra".'

'Sorry, Ellen? Not with you?'

'Both on the *Humphrey Carter Interviews* . . . programme with Zena Fitzpatrick . . . and in the video you recorded at the birthday lunch, Humph deliberately says that she brings "something extra" to any day. He's flaunting it. He's rubbing Niall's nose in the fact of the affair. On your video, Niall looks really upset at that point. You can imagine how Humph and Zena might have giggled in bed about their "something extra". It's very cruel.'

I had expected Kirsty to leap to her father's defence, but she was too caught up with a new thought. 'At the birthday lunch, when Niall was upset, so was Mum.'

'What do you mean?'

'It's not on the video, because I wasn't filming her at that moment, but she reacted badly when Humph mentioned Zena's *something extra*. She looked really upset.'

'Do you know why?'

'I think,' said Kirsty deliberately, 'that because she'd recently seen the unexplained "SE" references in the diaries, and because Humph so emphasized the "something extra" in his speech, it was at that moment, for the first time, Mum realized that he'd been having this long affair with Zena.'

Which, if Kirsty's analysis was right, might have given Theresa Carter a very good motive to murder her husband.

EIGHTEEN

Wanda Lyall was pleased to see me. There was no reproach in her response to my apologies for not having made it sooner. But that didn't stop me from feeling guilty.

She made some tea and I am glad to say I watched her eat one of the two-finger KitKats I'd brought with me. She did look rather emaciated. I again worried about her genuinely forgetting to eat.

I'm a great believer in serendipity. Or do I mean synchronicity? A combination of both, probably. But I find, if I'm trying to work something out – a SpaceWoman problem or a blocked criminal investigation – when I get one breakthrough, it is frequently followed by another. That was what happened that afternoon in Wanda's flat.

Though my mind was full of the Carter family, I didn't think I'd said anything about them to Wanda. I was wrong.

'When you were last here,' she said, 'you mentioned doing some work at Staddles.'

'Did I? I'd forgotten.'

'At the time, I didn't know where it was,' Wanda went on determinedly. 'Never heard of it. But I have since, with all the stuff there's been in the press about Humphrey Carter.'

'Ah. Right.'

'Terrible thing, a man like him topping himself, isn't it?'

I agreed it was. I certainly wasn't about to get involved in the complications of my own thoughts on the case.

'I used to enjoy his journalism,' Wanda said. 'Not so interested in his television stuff. But Humphrey Carter liked being controversial, he liked rubbing conventional people up the wrong way. I enjoy columnists who do that. Reminds me of the Duchess in *Alice in Wonderland.* Her song: "He only does it to annoy, because he knows it teases." Humphrey Carter was like that. A controversialist, a provocateur. He could be very funny with it.'

An exciting thought was forming in my head. 'If he was one of your favourite journalists, Wanda, does that mean you've still got some of his columns in the magazines you've kept?'

'It certainly does.' She moved across to the pine chest and opened it. 'I've been re-reading them a bit since I heard about his death.'

'Were these in *The Spectator*?'

'No, he did a lot for them, but that's not where he published his strongest pieces. The really good stuff was in a magazine called *Rant*.'

'I've heard of it,' I said. 'Humph was one of the people who set it up.'

'Yes, with some other like-minded troublemakers. They all loved shouting their mouths off. "Trenchant" is the word that could be used to describe them. Or "bloody-minded". Or, to some people, "deeply offensive".'

She found the copy she was looking for in the pine chest, opened it instinctively to the right page and offered it to me. 'This I thought was particularly interesting, Ellen. Especially given the verdict of suicide.'

I looked down at it. The page which I had last seen, whisky-stained, on Humph's desk, next to his dead body. Headed: 'COME IN, NUMBER EIGHTY – YOUR TIME IS UP!' The page which stated his intention to kill himself when he reached the age of eighty. The page which ended with the two paragraphs:

> I must confess my sleeping-pill-accompanying drink of choice would not be a wine. I like wine but I've always found that, for getting pissed, spirits are more effective. So, it'd be whisky for me. And not some posh, esoteric single malt. No, I'm not up myself. A common or garden blended whisky would do the job. Famous Grouse is the one I favour. I have very frequently fallen asleep following excesses of that. What more suitable tipple could there be to escort me into that magical sleep from which I do not wake?
>
> Come on, everyone, don't be greedy. Give a thought to the younger generation. Support voluntary euthanasia at eighty. You know it makes sense.

Except that wasn't where it ended. The article continued on the right-hand side of the centrefold, on a page that had not been present on Humph's desk. The supposed suicide note continued:

> Well, yes, that's the logic. It would, after all, be the altruistic thing to do. And if that's what you do want to do, don't let me stop you.
>
> However, it is not for me. In my case, so long as there's another lunch to be eaten, another bout of love with a woman, another bottle of wine or scotch to be drunk, another person to annoy . . . I'm going to go on living!

I was so full of the news that I rang Theresa the minute I got back to the Yeti. With some pride, I told her that we finally had proof Humph had been murdered. Someone had known that the suicidal content in the *Rant* article stopped conveniently with the end of a paragraph at the bottom of the page. Leaving the other two, defiantly optimistic paragraphs on the other side of the centrefold.

'Did you know about the article, Theresa?'

'No,' she replied. 'You've asked me this before, Ellen.'

'Humph didn't read it to you just after he'd written it?'

'He may well have done. But I have no recollection of it. We're talking many years ago.'

'Yes. Perhaps,' I suggested, 'you should look in Humph's study for the copy of the magazine it was taken from.'

'Yes, I probably should.' Theresa sounded fazed and distracted. 'The fact is, I keep putting off going into that room. It's still too full of Humph. I know I'll have to get round to it at some point, but I'm not going to do anything like that till after the funeral.'

'Very sensible,' I said. 'And, when you are ready to face it, perhaps I could be there too, so that it's not such a lonely task.' It wouldn't have been the first time I had helped a bereaved spouse face sorting through their dead partner's belongings. It was quite a common call for the services of SpaceWoman.

'Yes, I think I'd appreciate that,' said Theresa. 'But, as I say, I can't really think about it at the moment.'

'No. I understand. One thing . . .' I hesitated. 'Do you think we should tell the police about the article . . . you know, the fact that what they read as a suicide note was part of what's almost a manifesto against suicide?'

'Oh, I don't think so,' Theresa said promptly. 'Leave well enough alone. The police are always complaining about their workload and inadequate resources. With Humph, they've got the suicide verdict they wanted. I don't think we should add to their burden by stirring things up again.'

As I drove back home, I assessed the implications of the revelation in Wanda's flat. It did put a whole new emphasis on the murder scenario.

Humph was killed by someone who knew about the article he'd written for *Rant*. And presumably knew where to find it among the many papers in his study. Realistically – excluding the grandchildren for obvious reasons – there was a shortlist of five candidates. Theresa, Chloe, Kirsty, Garth or Niall.

Given Humph's pride in his own work and habit of showing new stuff to anyone who happened to be in range, it was entirely possible that he had shown the 'COME IN, NUMBER EIGHTY – YOUR TIME IS UP!' piece to his daughters. And, even if he hadn't, Kirsty, the self-appointed archivist of her father's career, would probably have known about it. She might well have mentioned the article to her waste-of-space husband Garth.

Niall Fitzpatrick had mentioned Humph reading out pieces of journalism to him. He'd also said that Theresa and the girls had frequently had to act as an audience for the stuff.

Theresa . . . Thinking about her made me rather uncomfortable. I had never had any doubt about the cause of Oliver's death, because I was the one who had found him asphyxiated in the car in the garage. But wouldn't most widows want the cause of their husband's demise to be officially recorded? Unless they had a particular reason for wanting the truth to remain hidden.

'Leave well enough alone,' Theresa had said. Why, though?

It was a strange request, but I had learned over the years never to question too much what Dodge asked me to do. He always had his reasons, though those reasons rarely conformed with other people's.

As instructed, I got there at eight o'clock in the morning. I left the Yeti in his yard and we set off in the 1951 Morris Commer

CV9/40 Tipper van. Dodge didn't tell me where we were going but, after a while, I recognized the route.

Work had been done on Mazz's caravan. The exterior now looked almost as good as the interior. Of course, there wasn't panelling on the outside, but the green mould had been scraped off and the whole thing painted white. The windows sparkled and the structure had been raised from the ground by the introduction of new tyres.

Dodge and Mazz didn't talk much, but they both knew exactly what they had to do. The Commer had been manoeuvred round the back of the derelict farmhouse till its towbar was nudging against the caravan's connector. The metal of this shone new. Dodge must have replaced the old one. In fact, it looked as if he'd made over the whole caravan to the high standards he'd applied to his precious 1951 Morris Commer CV9/40 Tipper van.

The coupling was smoothly effected, and soon the three of us were driving back to Dodge's place. He drove, I sat in the middle, with Mazz to my left. She smelled of Imperial Leather soap. This was how Dodge wanted us to travel. The deal was that they'd go back later to pick up Mazz's 1972 Ford Transit Mk1 Pick-Up.

The two of them didn't speak and I knew better than to try to make conversation. But, in spite of the silence, there was something almost triumphant about our progress through the lanes of West Sussex.

Soon enough, the Commer, with caravan in tow, turned in at Dodge's gateway. A bit more manoeuvring ensued, until the caravan was in its designated spot, on the edge of the courtyard, between Dodge's workshop/living quarters and the house from which Mazz had stolen his wood. There was no discussion about where the caravan should be sited. That must have been decided in a previous conversation. So, although there was little evidence of it that morning, the pair of them must have talked sometimes.

Once the caravan was in place to the – unspoken – satisfaction of both of them, Dodge opened the door with a gesture that was almost chivalric and gestured to Mazz to enter. She went inside and closed the door behind her.

Dodge turned to me. 'I'll take you home now,' he said, his eyes as ever scouting out my shoes.

Nothing was said on the way back to Chichester. When I was on the pavement outside my house, Dodge mumbled, 'Thank you for your help.' And drove off.

My *help*? What had I done?

And yet, in a strange way, I knew. What had happened that morning was a momentous event in Dodge's life. Possibly in Mazz's too.

And he'd needed someone else there, to kind of validate the experience.

It was the first time in my life I had taken on the role of a chaperone.

I made myself a cheese and ham omelette for lunch and tried to find a subject I was happy to think about. Jools seemed to be in a better place but, to avoid deep pain, I had to keep my mind off Ben. Thinking of Fleur and Kenneth wasn't going to improve my mood. And, as for allowing my suspicions about Theresa to develop . . . well, I didn't want to go there.

So, I tried to think of other factors in the story of Humph's death that might exonerate her. I didn't write notes with lists of suspects, motives and so on. Only people in detective fiction do that. Real people never do.

But I tried to remember if there was any clue, any hint, any bit of conversation I'd heard, whose relevance I had yet to configure.

I seemed to have seen a lot of people over the last few weeks. Some from my world, some from very different worlds. Layla Valdez, Sydnee, Mr Kumari . . . And what was the name of that producer I met in Chloe Carter's dressing room? Gwen . . . Gwen Something . . .? Gwen Stefani? No, she's a singer. But the second name was something foreign-sounding . . .

Martino! That was it. Gwen Martino. Chloe Carter's producer friend was called Gwen Martino.

I tried to recall what she had said in the dressing room before Chloe pointed out that I was there. Something about some project being greenlighted . . .? Something that would be a big break for Chloe . . .?

It's probably never been easier than it is now to find out about people. Complete nobodies advertise themselves on Facebook and other platforms. And it's hard to escape those in the public eye, constantly self-glorifying online.

So, I had no trouble finding out more about Gwen Martino.

Before checking out her social media posts, I googled and found her website. Or rather, the website for her company. Called Dry Martino Films. I quite liked that.

Gwen herself headed the list on the page entitled 'Team'. It was not a world with which I could claim much familiarity, but she seemed to have been busily employed by the BBC and many independent companies before setting up on her own. I hadn't heard of any of the programmes she'd been involved in but that didn't surprise me. Even though a lot of Dry Martino Films I'd never heard of had been nominated for awards I'd never heard of.

The area of the website that proved fruitful for my enquiries, however, was the page called *In Development*. The number of projects seemed limitless – original dramas, adaptations of crime novels, quiz formats, chat shows and documentaries. Even I, knowing little about show business, could see that very few of them would ever reach the screen.

The bit of *In Development* which interested me, however, was headed *Breaking News*.

'LIFE-TAKERS – docuseries about the increasing number of suicides in the UK, what causes them and what can be done about them. Presented by Chloe Carter, for whom the subject has a particular resonance as her father, the chat show host Humphrey Carter, recently took his own life.'

The strong impression I'd got from Chloe was that she'd do anything to further her career in television. Even to the point of murdering her father?

Theresa Carter had suggested I should 'leave well enough alone'. But that didn't stop me from texting her a link to the Dry Martino Films website.

NINETEEN

The day of the funeral was cold but, thank God, not raining. Theresa got her way, and it was a small affair. Family only, plus Humph's two agents, as well as Niall Fitzpatrick and me. Kirsty and Garth – or, more likely, Kirsty on her own – had decided that the grandchildren would only be upset by the occasion. Pick-ups from school and playdates had been arranged for them, so that their parents wouldn't have to rush back.

I was surprised when Theresa told me on the phone that the service would take advantage of a crematorium's anonymity.

'But should it be there, if you're suspicious that Humph was murdered?'

'What do you mean, Ellen?'

'I know the police have released the body, but if there was ever a need for further investigation, you can't exhume ashes. Well, you can, but you're not going to get much information from them.'

'There never will be "need for further investigation",' Theresa had said firmly.

Leave well enough alone. She was virtually saying it again. And who cares if cremation destroys all the evidence?

Though, when I came to think about the situation rationally, Theresa's decision didn't seem so perverse. All of the post-mortem tests must have been performed on the cadaver of Humphrey Carter. There was no argument about the cause of death. The point at issue was whether he had mixed the sleeping pills in the Famous Grouse himself, or whether someone else had done it. No further post-mortem tests could decide that. Unless there had been a hidden witness or video camera in the study at Staddles, the precise sequence of events could only ever be guessed at. And Theresa, perhaps from sheer exhaustion, seemed to have given up guessing.

Given what I now knew about the 'Life-Takers' project, I wondered whether she too had any thoughts about the guilt of her older daughter. I wondered whether she'd followed up on the Dry Martino Films website. She certainly hadn't mentioned the link I'd sent her.

I looked at the pair of them, sitting side by side in the crematorium. The clergyman, who'd heard of Humphrey Carter but never met him, was intoning platitudes about his loss. And, for the first time, I saw a likeness between Theresa and Chloe. Something about the set of their jaws, the lines of determination, showed them both to be formidable combatants. Not women to be taken lightly.

I still hadn't worked Theresa out. She nearly fitted one stereotype: the talented artiste who'd put her own career on hold to support her husband's and to bring up their children. But in no way did she appear as a victim. There was a steeliness about her, evident in her reaction – or lack of reaction – to Humph's death. It had also been there in her conviction that he had been murdered and her determination to find the perpetrator. A determination which seemed to have melted away since the coroner's verdict of suicide.

What would happen, though, if I managed to prove the killer's identity? When I told Theresa the name, would she feel obliged to take my evidence to the police? To exact some kind of private revenge? Or would she follow her stated intention to 'leave well enough alone'.

And if someone were to suggest to her the possibility that Chloe had killed her father to advance her television career, how would Theresa react?

What went on behind that highly polished exterior was unknowable, certainly to me – and possibly to everyone else.

I looked round the little group in the chapel. The two agents had done their jobs well. No news of the funeral's timing had been leaked to the media. Or was the lack of public in the crematorium just another reflection of the fact that Humphrey Carter was 'yesterday's man'? How that would have annoyed him if he had been around to know about it.

I wasn't sure how I should proceed. I had the uncomfortable certainty that home truths were going to be spoken soon. But they somehow wouldn't have seemed proper in the crematorium chapel.

The curtains followed their time-honoured choreography and closed around the coffin of Humphrey Carter.

Theresa Carter, the consummate hostess, had of course provided the perfect lunch which was ready and waiting in the Aga when the funeral party returned to Staddles. In deference to the chilly weather, there was a Thai Green Chicken Curry with an array of elegant extras. Eton Mess for dessert.

We ate in the kitchen. That somehow felt less formal. Also, I wondered, was it to avoid direct comparisons with the last time many of the same personnel had gathered round the dining room table for Humph's birthday lunch?

On a surface by the Aga were lined up more bottles of Humph's favourite Bordeaux than could possibly be consumed by so small a party.

For the usual reasons, I restricted myself to one glass. Chloe stuck to water because she was driving and as concerned about losing her licence as I was. 'It's just the kind of story the tabloids would love,' she said. 'TV STAR DRUNK AT THE WHEEL.'

No one questioned her self-description. Maybe, I thought, daytime presenters are classified as 'TV Stars'. What did I know of that world?

It was perhaps not strange how much we were all aware of Humph's absence. The kitchen seemed empty without his huge personality dominating affairs. The short figure of Niall Fitzpatrick was an inadequate substitute. As perhaps he had been throughout his long relationship with Humphrey Carter.

Thank God for Humph's literary and television agents Their presence at the wake was a blessing. I may have been something of a catalyst too. Outsiders kept the family from too much internal sniping. And from talking about things that mattered.

The agents were also extremely entertaining. They were being picked up by a hire car, so had no inhibitions about downing large quantities of the Bordeaux. They went into a practised routine, full of showbiz stories and scandalous gossip. Chloe joined avidly in the bitchiness, asserting the wideness of her media circle. Niall and Theresa were still close enough to that world to contribute the occasional memory or anecdote.

I was so relieved not to have Fleur there. It was exactly the kind of gossipfest she would have loved to dominate (no matter how much she was embarrassing her daughter).

So, the conversation flowed. Though, occasionally, there was an affectionate reference to Humph, the atmosphere remained light-hearted. But there was still about the lunch a sense of something less pleasant looming. The agents' hire car was coming to pick them up at two. Then the family gloves would be off.

After the agents had had what they called 'pivotal pees' to last them the journey back to London, they left. Suddenly, Staddles seemed very quiet. And I knew that, soon, I would have to say something.

The next to excuse themselves were the Wickenses, Kirsty announced that they had 'to get back for the kids' and no one objected. Hugs were exchanged. Kirsty gave extravagant ones to Niall and Theresa, who sent 'lots of love to Justin and Molly.' Kirsty gave me an intense hug. There was a beseeching look in her eyes, as if she expected something of me, that I had to sort things out for her.

All Chloe got from her sister was a little opening-and-closing-hand mime. Garth was more flamboyant. He gave Niall one of those male hugs that men are still not very good at, arms over shoulders and no contact with the lower body. His hug for Theresa was of the protesting-too-much kind, expressing a closeness between them that didn't really exist. His embrace of Chloe was more full-on, suggesting that he quite liked the idea of snogging a 'TV Star'. He decided he didn't know me well enough to justify a hug. To my considerable relief.

Garth had been treating himself generously to the Bordeaux and, as they reached the front door, he said to Kirsty, 'You'll drive, won't you?'

The look on her face as she agreed offered excellent shorthand for the state of their marriage.

That left four of us in Staddles. Including the murderer of Humphrey Carter.

Theresa had produced more perfect coffee. We sat round the kitchen table. I didn't think I could avoid starting much longer, so I blundered in.

'I think we all have reservations about the coroner's verdict on Humph, don't we?'

'Do we?' Chloe Carter sounded genuinely shocked by what I'd said. But then she had inherited performance skills from both of her parents. I had seen her projecting false emotions on television. And the coroner's verdict had supplied her passport to presenting the 'Life-Takers' series. So, it was in her interests not to have any reservations.

'Well, I certainly do,' I said doggedly.

Theresa sighed, as if in response to a troublesome child. 'Yes, and we've established that you're a terrier, aren't you, Ellen? Won't let go of an idea, will you?'

'Maybe not. But come on, you think the same, don't you, Theresa?'

Another weary sigh. 'Yes. For what it's worth, I think he probably was murdered.'

Again, the look which Chloe directed at her mother was a very convincing expression of surprise.

'What about you, Niall?'

'Ellen, I have considered the possibility,' he replied cautiously. 'Obviously, I have. You lose one of your best friends, you consider every possible explanation. But, having been through them all endlessly, I still think the coroner got it right.'

Chloe spoke. 'Look, can we stop this conversation?' There was a new tone in her voice, something more naked, perhaps with a hint of desperation. 'I've lost my father. The idea that he felt so badly about life, so badly about his friends and family, that he killed himself is already pretty appalling. The fanciful idea that he was murdered just muddies the waters and makes everything worse!'

She really did sound on the edge of tears now. Once again I reminded myself of her performance skills.

'Chloe,' said Theresa, 'do you deny that Humph's death was extremely convenient for you?'

'What do you mean?'

'The timing of it made you a shoo-in as presenter of Gwen Martino's "Life-Takers" series.'

So, Theresa had followed the link. Chloe looked at her mother with surprise and an element of respect. 'How do you know about that?'

'It's trumpeted on the Dry Martino Films website.'

'Ah. I didn't know Gwen had posted it so quickly. We only got the green light yesterday.'

'I don't know what you're talking about,' Niall complained plaintively.

'The details don't matter at the moment,' Theresa said, rather sharply. She looked her daughter straight in the eyes and said, 'Humph had diminished you all your life. He'd dismissed all your professional achievements as worthless. He made no secret of the fact that he preferred Kirsty to you. You could never be good enough for him. And, over the years, the fantasy grew in your mind of how much easier your life would be without Humph in it.'

Chloe looked at her mother with an expression of incredulity. 'Are you suggesting that I killed him to further my television career?'

'That's exactly what I'm suggesting. You've had a lot of success but none of it has been fully satisfying, because there was always one vital component lacking. Humph's approval. You knew you were never going to get that while he was alive.'

'So, I killed him?'

'Yes,' said Theresa relentlessly.

I was surprised at the direction the dialogue was taking. Chloe's reaction to the accusation was so different from what I'd expected.

'Oh, Mum,' she said, 'you have got things totally so wrong. You've never understood what my relationship with Humph was. You're right, he was always diminishing me. He never left me in any doubt that he preferred Kirsty to me. All of that is true. But what you don't understand is that all of that is what made me love him.

'Yes, ours was a very combative relationship, but both of us loved combat. That was the dynamo that kept us going. It's what gave me the motivation for my career. It made me want to achieve the impossible. To make Humph proud of me!

'Now he's gone, it's like my motivation's gone with him. I should be ecstatic about the "Life-Takers" series. It's a real breakthrough in my career. It takes me from just a smirking daytime presenter to someone who's taken seriously as a jour-nalist. And yet now . . . I've even contemplated turning it down.

Because what's the point of my making a series like that without Humph seeing it?

'Oh, Mum, you've never understood how my mind works, have you? I've been worried for years about what would happen to my drive, my impetus, my motivation when Humph finally died. If you think I would contemplate helping him on his way . . . well, you couldn't be more wrong.

'And the knowledge that I couldn't save him, that my love, the family's love, wasn't enough to stop him from taking his own life . . . that's something I'm going to have to live with for the rest of mine.'

There was a silence after this impassioned speech. Then Chloe announced, 'I must get back to London.' She went across to plant a dry kiss on her mother's cheek. 'Talk on the phone soon.'

'Yes.'

'And to know that you could actually think that of me . . . that you could imagine I would have killed Humph . . .' Chloe ran out of words.

She picked up again with, 'Bye, Niall.' No intonation. Certainly, no hug.

She didn't even look at me. But, as she left the kitchen into the hall, I made no attempt to stop her. The scene hadn't played out exactly as I'd expected, but it had provided me with the information I required.

We heard the front door close with some force. I looked from Theresa to Niall.

'I think we need more wine,' said the widow. She opened one of the bottles by the Aga. Looked at me. I shook my head. She poured Bordeaux into the other two glasses.

'Well . . .' said Theresa Carter. 'It seems that we need to talk.' She addressed Niall. 'You and I haven't really had this discussion but Ellen and I are convinced that Humph was murdered.'

'Oh?' He sounded light-hearted. 'And what do you base this on? Do you have any of that old-fashioned evidence stuff.'

Theresa looked at me. 'Do you have anything I don't know about?'

'Maybe. I think I probably have stuff that Niall doesn't know about.'

He spread his hands wide. 'Well, please fill me in,' he said. Still easy-going but maybe with an edge of caution.

'All right. Well, let's start with the so-called *suicide note* . . .'

'OK.'

'It turns out that what was left on Humph's desk was not the complete article he had written.'

'Oh?' Niall sounded puzzled.

'Conveniently, it finished at the bottom of the page, with a full stop. And, at that point, it seemed Humph was genuinely recommending suicide at the age of eighty.'

'That's what he was recommending,' Niall protested.

'No. On the next page, at the end of the article, he took it all back, said he was going to live as long as he possibly could, "so long as there's another lunch to be eaten, another bout of love with a woman, another bottle of wine or scotch to be drunk, another person to annoy."'

'Ah,' said Niall. 'That sounds like Humph.'

'Yes,' Theresa agreed.

'Niall,' I said, 'you told me that Humph often shared his journalism with you. He'd show you bits he'd just written.'

'He was always desperate for an audience.'

'So, do you remember this "COME IN, NUMBER EIGHTY – YOUR TIME IS UP!" article?'

He gave a strange look. 'Good Lord, no.'

'I knew about it,' said Theresa quietly.

I was taken aback. Her words contradicted what she'd told me on the phone when I revealed the discovery I'd made in Wanda Lyall's flat.

'I know about quite a lot more than you imagine, Ellen.' She looked at Niall. 'More than you imagine too.'

'Oh?' he said.

'Are you saying, Theresa,' I asked, 'that you know what caused Humph's death?'

'Oh no. I don't know all of it.'

I was in a bit of a dilemma. The one thing I hadn't told either of them yet was what I had worked out about the entries in Humph's appointments diaries, because the information might be hurtful to Theresa. But I reckoned I'd have to risk that collateral damage.

'You know Kirsty had been looking through Humph's old diaries . . .?'

Theresa nodded and Niall said, 'No, I didn't. I didn't know he kept a diary.'

He looked at Theresa for amplification. 'Just an appointments one,' she said.

He shrugged. 'Well, he kept it to himself. I never saw it.'

'Anyway,' I went on, 'there were a series of regular appointments that he marked simply with the initials "SE".'

'Ah,' said Niall. 'I think I know where this is going.'

'I think I do too,' said Theresa.

If she knew, then there was no need for caution on my part. 'SE, I'm pretty sure, was Humph's shorthand for "something extra".'

'Yes,' said Niall. 'It meant a date with his long-term mistress.' He looked towards Theresa, fearful of her reaction.

But she met the situation with her customary serenity. 'I had worked that out.'

She rose from the kitchen table. 'Kirsty brought the diaries back this morning. I'll go and get them. See if we can find any more clues as to who the mysterious lover was.'

As she left the room and set off upstairs, Niall and I looked at each other in amazement.

'She really doesn't know?' I asked.

'Seems not,' said Niall.

'But if she didn't make the connection between the *something extra* and Zena – which is what Kirsty reckoned she must have done – then Theresa didn't have a motive to kill him.'

'She had worked out from the diaries that he had a long-running affair. She just didn't know who with. Still, the fact of her husband having an affair might have triggered a homicidal impulse inside her.'

'Do you really believe that, Niall?'

'No.' He shrugged. 'No, I don't, really. Amazingly, though, it seems that Theresa still doesn't know that her husband and my wife had an affair that lasted more than thirty years.'

'The wife, traditionally, being "the last to know".'

'And the cuckolded husband,' Niall said wryly, 'knowing all along. Knowing that the cuckolder even put their assignations in his appointments diary as *something extra*.'

He picked up the bottle of Bordeaux. A look in my direction got a predictable shake of the head. He filled up his glass.

'So, what still remains unresolved,' I said to him, 'is the exact circumstances of Humph's death.'

'Oh, that,' Niall said casually, as if it were a matter of minor importance. 'I killed him.'

'Really?'

'By the method that everyone seems to have worked out . . . except perhaps for the police and the coroner. Of course I remembered the "COME IN, NUMBER EIGHTY – YOUR TIME IS UP!" article. I even thought at the time how well it could work as a suicide note. I knew where to find the copy in Humph's study. I knew about the Famous Grouse and the sleeping pills. Yes, I did it.'

Never, I thought, had a confession of murder been so matter-of-fact.

'But why?' I asked. 'I'm not asking what your motive was. Humph was clearly a bastard who screwed you in every way possible.'

'Including screwing my wife for good measure,' he suggested. '*Something extra.*'

'All right. But why, after years of humiliation, did you kill him on his eightieth birthday? Was there some reason for that date?'

'Not for the date particularly,' said Niall. 'But there was a reason. A reason that made sense to me. All right, Humph had treated me as a whipping boy from when we first met. He has, as you say, humiliated me, not least by stealing away the wife whom I absolutely adored. But I kind of got used to that. I could live with it. Zena and I still spent a lot of time together. We loved each other. We shared a qualified happiness, even though I knew she loved another man. But with Humph that was just sex, anyway. We had something more than that.'

'So, what happened?'

'Zena died,' he replied simply.

'Why did that make the situation between you and Humph change?'

'It changed because he showed absolutely no sadness, no sense of bereavement. I, the one who'd been excluded from her bed for many years, was totally destroyed by her death. And yet the man who had been her lover for over thirty years, the man she had loved, seemed to be completely unaffected. Humph just continued in his own, selfish way.

'Not only that. He made a joke of it. At the birthday lunch, teasing me with the "something extra" reference. Talking of Zena as one of the things we had *shared*. The fact he could say those things made me realize that he'd never loved Zena. Never with the love that means really caring about another person. But she'd loved him. She had given him her precious love, the love which would have meant so much if she had granted it to me. And, for Humph, that was just something to make jokes about.

'I couldn't stand that. So, I killed him.' Again, the confession was completely undramatic.

Niall Fitzpatrick took a long draught of red wine, then grinned across at me. What he was about to say I never knew, because at that moment Theresa arrived back in the kitchen with the diaries. Niall said he'd better be getting home, and went.

Theresa seemed unsurprised that I hadn't followed his example.

'Niall's just confessed to me that he murdered Humph,' I announced.

'Ah.' Never had a single word been weighted with so little intonation.

'But I don't believe him,' I said.

'Oh?' Then, casually, 'Why not?'

'Because of some things he said. Because of some things you said.'

'Elucidate,' she said coolly.

'Way back, just after I'd found Humph's body, you mentioned the case of Cedric Waites, the hoarder in Chichester who I discovered had been murdered. I didn't think it odd at the time, but in retrospect it was a rather strange thing to be talking about at such a moment.'

Theresa Carter gave no reaction.

'Thinking about it since, I've realized that already you were lining me up as a potential investigator. You were worried that the police would find out the real circumstances of the murder, so you set me up to see whether I could work that out for myself. Only, when the suicide verdict was announced did you no longer need my services. From then on, you recommended that I should "leave well enough alone".'

'Yes,' said Theresa, grimly amused, 'but you wouldn't, would you?'

'No, I wouldn't. I'm afraid I'd got the bit between my teeth by then.'

'You certainly had. I've used the word *terrier* before. You're hard to shake off.'

'I'll take that as a compliment.'

'It is one. I'm afraid I had engaged the services of a rather more intelligent investigator than I had intended.' A deep, weary sigh. 'What tipped you off, Ellen? I must obviously be a bit more canny when I commit my next murder.'

'I suppose the main thing that made me suspicious was the suddenness with which you lost interest in the investigation once the coroner had given a verdict of suicide.'

'Hm. I must be a bit subtler next time,' she said, as if making an elaborate mental note. 'Anything else?'

'Something you did only about half an hour ago. Here in this kitchen. I'd sent you the link to the Dry Martino Films website. The fact that you used the information you found there to accuse Chloe . . . that told me you thought I was getting too close to the truth.'

She nodded rueful acknowledgement. 'Yes, wasn't very subtle, was it? It's just . . . you'd offered me a potential get-out and I knew that Chloe's got a hide like a rhinoceros, so . . .'

I wondered if, after her daughter's recent display of emotion, she still felt that.

'Anyway,' Theresa went on, 'going back to Humph's murder . . . Ooh, I get something of a *frisson* saying that . . . what you want to know is . . . what's that expression they always use, Ellen? Oh yes, what "tipped me over the edge"?'

'Kirsty gave me the answer to that.'

'Oh, really? How?'

'She told me that, when Humph, at his birthday lunch, used the expression "something extra", Niall looked really upset. She said that, though the camera wasn't on you, you looked

very upset too. I think, because you'd been going through
Humph's diaries for the proposed memoir, because you'd been
puzzling over the meaning of the constant repetition of the
initials "SE", they suddenly made sense to you. And, from the
brazen, boastful way Humph used the words, and the way he
talked about "sharing" with Niall, you also knew, with horrifying
clarity, what they meant – that your husband had been having
a long-term affair with your best friend. And that is why you
murdered him.'

The kitchen filled with a long, long silence.

Then, Theresa Carter said, 'I'm rather touched by the fact that
Niall confessed to the murder. Covering up for me – what a
gentleman. He knew from the start that I'd killed Humph. When
he woke up, the Monday morning after the birthday lunch, he
went into the study. I found him in there. He knew what'd
happened. We talked.'

'Yes, that was another inconsistency I discovered.'

'What do you mean, Ellen?'

'You said you'd seen Niall that morning. He said he'd not
seen anyone that morning.'

'Ah.' She took on an expression of rueful self-criticism. 'I'm
really not cut out for this murder game, you know.'

Another long silence before she resumed, 'So, not a very
original scenario, is it? The old cliché of the wife "being the last
to know". And "hell having no fury . . ." What corny expressions.
Shabby, tabloid words, aren't they? Even though one of them is
a quote from Congreve.' She took an elegant sip of wine.
Everything she did was always elegant. 'Well, Ellen, you have
the great satisfaction of being right. The question now is . . .
what are you going to do about it?'

I left Staddles soon after, without elaborate farewells. I wondered
what would happen between Theresa and Niall when they next
talked. She had confessed to me that she'd murdered Humph.
Something that Niall had known all the time. And he'd confessed
to the crime, in the chivalrous hope of diverting my suspicions
away from her.

Theresa hadn't seemed worried that I might go to the police
with what I now knew. Which showed her to be a good judge

of character. I believe in justice, but not necessarily justice as defined in courts of law. The justice I believe in is the one where the right thing happens.

TWENTY

After the chilly misery of February and March, the change to Summer Time offered the hope of longer evenings. I was surprised to have a call from Dodge. I hadn't been in touch since the great ceremony of the caravan-moving. He asked me to join 'them' that evening, as 'they' had something to show me.

It was an outside table with four chairs, all made to the highest standard of woodworking. 'We made it together,' said Dodge.

Mazz didn't say anything. She rarely did.

The caravan was on the edge of the yard, exactly where it had been deposited. Its bodywork still sparkled, and a small garden had been planted in a rectangle around its plot. It formed a nice symmetry with the 1951 Morris Commer CV9/40 Tipper van on the other side.

Whatever he may have done back in his City days, Dodge didn't drink alcohol now. He produced nettle tea for the three of us. The weather was just warm enough to sit comfortably on the new furniture and sip away.

At one point, Mazz, who had a slight cold, announced she must get a clean handkerchief. 'Got one under my pillow,' she said and went into the caravan to fetch it.

The implication from this was that she still had her own accommodation. Their sleeping arrangements were not my concern. There are as many relationships as there are couples and who am I to pontificate on which ones are right or wrong or better or worse than the others? Finding someone with whom you can share at least part of your life is so difficult that the identity or orientation of that person is a mere detail.

What mattered was that, with Mazz, Dodge seemed to have made contact with another human being. And maybe that was part of a healing process for both of them.

*　　*　　*

Fleur's husband Kenneth got the results of his latest tests. His blood pressure was worryingly high. He had been advised to stop playing golf. My first unworthy thought was that this might be potentially good news for me. With Kenneth around the house, maybe his wife would be less dependent on her daughter at weekends?

The relief was short-lived. My mother, predictably enough, turned the results of the tests into a three-act drama. If 'something happened' to Kenneth, how on earth would she manage on her own?

This question came accompanied by a worrying implication. That, of course, Fleur Bonnier wouldn't be on her own. Because she'd have a dutiful daughter to spend more time with her. To look after her. Wouldn't she?

Relations with my daughter remained fragile but OK. Cohabiting worked, more or less, because we didn't see that much of each other. And the working relationship in SpaceWoman was good. I bought a very cheap second-hand Skoda Fabia for Jools. Which made her job a lot easier.

Increasingly, Jools was getting bookings on her own initiative, independent of me. Which was the way I had hoped things would go. But I still wanted to get her terms of employment on a more official basis. I wanted to know how permanent or temporary our current arrangement was. Jools was reluctant to discuss such matters.

The Worthing connection seemed to be ongoing, but she had still given me no indication as to who it was she was seeing there. Which was her prerogative, I guess. I certainly didn't want to be a snooping mother but the odd detail – like a name, say – wouldn't have come amiss.

I devoutly buttoned my lip and made no enquiries. Jools would tell me what was happening in her own good time.

Then, rather to my surprise, she did. One April evening, I had only just got in from a day's decluttering when Jools arrived in the kitchen with a bottle of Merlot. 'Let's open this, Mum,' she said, 'and have a talk.'

Though they were the words I had been hoping to hear from

her for a long time, I still approached the encounter with some trepidation. We sat opposite each other at the kitchen table, both in our SpaceWoman polo shirts, and raised our glasses to each other.

'I've been thinking a lot,' said Jools who had definitely spent time preparing for this meeting. 'Our current situation is unsatisfactory in many ways.'

The temptation to ask why was strong but I curbed it. Let her construct the narrative in her own way, without any prompts from me.

'We need,' she went on, 'to sort out where I stand with SpaceWoman, you know, whether I'm going to be doing it permanently or if I should move on to something else.'

Exactly the subject I had wanted to raise. But I still said nothing.

'And I think I have a solution . . . well, an action plan, anyway. I've been in touch with Perry Driscoll.'

'Ah. Have you?' That was something I didn't know.

'Yes. And don't worry, I'm not taking any more money from him. He's stopped all the standing orders. More importantly, though, I've got him to realize that he has a problem.'

'The hoarding, you mean?'

'Yes. Your analysis of his personality was spot on, Mum. He has at least three other flats as full of stuff as the Herne Hill one.'

'Has he let you inside any of them?'

'Almost. The Herne Hill one. He did actually open the door and let me see how narrow the pathways were to his bedroom and bathroom.'

'That's a great sign of trust,' I said. 'For a hoarder to let anyone into their space – or perhaps I should say *lack of space*.'

'Yes, I reckoned that, Mum. If he's beginning to trust me, I might be able to help him.'

'How would you set about it?'

'My plan is,' Jools said, now slightly nervous to be putting her idea into words, 'that I should move back to Herne Hill and set up a kind of London branch of SpaceWoman.' As if afraid I might interrupt, she said hastily, 'And start it with Perry Driscoll as my first client.'

She took a long sip of wine, anxious about my reaction.

Which was as positive as she could have wished. 'I think that's a great idea, Jools.'

With relief, her words tumbled out, 'And, you see, Perry would pay for my services, or we'd set the charges against what I owe him for the mortgage payments and everything else and then we . . .' She ran out of talk and looked to me for more validation.

'I think it's terrific,' I said. 'We can sort out how we actually work it from the business side. You could continue being an employee of SpaceWoman, though actually I'd rather we became partners in the company. Lots of ways we can sort that out. I'll get on to our solicitor first thing tomorrow.'

'That'd be great.' Jools paused for a moment, then blushed. 'Actually, there's something else . . .'

'Oh yes?'

'You know I've been seeing someone in Worthing.'

'I know you've been spending a lot of time in Worthing.'

'Right, well . . . I met him when I was sorting out that student house.'

'I remember.'

'And, well, he's not actually a student. I mean he graduated last year, and he's been doing odd jobs round Worthing while applying for proper jobs. And now he's got one. London-based, quite good money.'

I might have asked what kind of job, but I didn't. Two minutes before I had had no confirmation Jools actually was seeing someone in Worthing. Now I knew that she was and that he was male. I didn't want to rush her.

'So, what we're planning, Mum, is he should come and stay with me in Herne Hill. And he'd pay me rent, which would help defray expenses. And we'd . . . um . . . see how things work out.'

'It sounds a very good idea, Jools.'

'Oh,' she said shyly. 'His name's Tariq.'

'Have you looked at today's *Showbizzy Beez*?'

'No, Fleur, I haven't. I've been busy.'

'She's gone back to Brad Forelli!'

'What? Who? What are you talking about, Fleur?'

'It's in today's *Showbizzy Beez*.'

'Oh, do you still look at that?'

'Of course I do. I'm waiting to see something about me.'

'Something about you?'

'Yes, but there hasn't been anything yet. Which is strange, because I've sent Sydnee lots of information about what I'm up to.'

'"Sydnee"? What, "Sydnee", as in Layla Valdez's publicist? She didn't say she'd represent you, did she?'

'Not in so many words,' said Fleur. 'But it was, kind of, implicit in our conversation. I gave her all my contact details.'

There are times when the size of my mother's ego can still surprise me. But it wasn't the moment to point out the unlikelihood of a Hollywood publicist helping along the career of a superannuated British actress. Instead, I asked, 'Anyway, what was it you saw in *Showbizzy Beez*?'

'Like I said, they're an item again.' She read down the phone to me, '"Hoopmeister Brad Forelli didn't have to wait too long for Layla Valdez to come running back to him. The ecstatic couple were seen all over each other at LA's swanky Cormorant Club. The Brit bombshell announced, *This time it's for keeps!*' Didn't you know that, Ellen?'

I had to admit that I didn't.

'Ben hasn't been in touch?'

'No.'

'Well, what do you think about it, Ellen?'

'I suppose . . . I suppose . . . I don't know whether the break-up is a good thing or a bad thing, but I suppose I worry about how Ben will have reacted.'

'Oh, I'd worry about that too,' said Fleur, 'except that all my worrying capacity is taken up at the moment with worrying about Kenneth.'

I was surprised to get a business call from Theresa Carter. Once again, she needed my SpaceWoman services and we made an appointment for me to return to Staddles. Now, she was no longer planning to move, but a major reorganization of the interior was necessary. The job would also involve the decluttering of The Hayes, where Niall and Zena Fitzpatrick had lived.

Because Niall was moving into Staddles with Theresa.

Well, why wouldn't it work? They'd known each other since they were at RADA. Their children had grown up together. They had lots of mutual friends. And they were both single.

I didn't think, in their future together, they'd probably talk much about the major figure in both of their lives, Humphrey Carter. Or about the circumstances of his death.

Relationships can be strengthened by shared secrets.

Later the same day, my mobile rang. I recognized the number instantly.

'Ma,' said Ben, 'I'm in a bad place.'